Assassinations

the Collected stories of Renate Yates

ASSASSINATIONS: the Collected Stories of Renate Yates

Copyright 2017 Renate Yates

Svengali Press
PO Box 1852
Strawberry Hills
NSW 2012
AUSTRALIA
&

ETT Imprint
PO Box R1906
Royal Exchange
NSW 1225
AUSTRALIA

ISBN 978-0-9942765-0-6 (p/b)
ISBN 978-1-925706-10-9 (e)

CONTENTS

ACKNOWLEDGEMENTS

My thanks go first to the late Geoffrey Dutton - (of fond memory) who published many of my first stories in the then Bulletin Literary Supplement.

Also to Stephen Knight editor of "Crimes for a Summer Christmas" and to Michael Wilding and David Myers (editors) for including me in their "Best Stories Under the Sun" series two and three.

Thanks too, to Gretchen Poiner for her splendid cactus arrangement which appears on the cover.

Thanks to my husband Tim who had the original idea for the cover and to Peter Jeffery and my daughter Emily who realised it so beautifully.

And my very special thanks to Sandra Darroch of Svengali Press for editing and publishing this collection.

To Tim, Nicholas and Emily

THE PERFECT MURDER

SHE LAY quite still in the darkness, listening intently, aware of the silence of the night but driving off the sleep she craved. Alert and watchful, she planned her next move, a simple, a necessary murder – a murder too important to allow herself the indulgence, now, of sleep.

Outside the night was a cold one; a sharp wind stirred the leaves but the stars were alive and glinting in the icy blackness. Restlessly she rose and paced the floor, willing the time to pass, waiting impatiently for the dawn. The two small figures by the window breathed steadily as they slept, unaware of their mother's preoccupations. They trusted her as children do, certain that no harm could come to them while she was there. Though when it happened that she was compelled to leave them alone, something she hated to do, it was never for long. And she never returned without a present for them both; a surprise, usually a delicacy of some kind to please them. Then, as mothers do, she would watch over them as they ate, ensuring that they grew as they should, healthy, with strong bones. Her ways with the two of them were invariably loving, always gentle and tender. They did not know that she could be cruel, that in certain situations she could be utterly heartless, at times even merciless. Later they would see it for themselves but not yet, not while they were still so small, so vulnerable.

Towards dawn she slept a little but her sleep was light and fitful, her dreams violent; she awoke suddenly, grateful to be free of them, it was vital, the murder she planned there in the darkness; the darkness that was lifting now with the first glimmerings of dawn. She looked down at the small sleeping forms, at the pale faces so peaceful in the half-light. Her conscience did not trouble her. The rewards implicit in the deed outweighed its hazards, outweighed its dangers.

Soon it would be day. Her body tautened with the thought but her eyes became calm. The decision had been made long ago – to carry it out successfully was all that remained.

When the little ones awoke, their blue eyes wide and eager their mother gave them a drink but ate nothing herself. Later, when the deed was accomplished would be time enough for her own needs.
She waited until the sun was up before she left them, knowing she would soon return. She was sure that they were quite safe together. Content, they played happily alone, still innocent.

Purposefully then, she walked out of the garden, across the road and towards the children's playground in the park. The swings, roundabouts and slides were set in sand to soften the children's falls. Large trees, eucalypts and wattles, gave shade and many flowerbeds with poppies, primulas and sweet-smelling stocks were bright around the perimeter. Here and there dumps of scarlet grevilleas attracted the birds who darted and chattered in their branches oblivious to the children's laughter and noise. Perhaps they were used to it.

Today there were not so many children in the park. It was earlier than usual; she had planned it thus. The absence of the regular crowd, those who came rowdily after school, pleased her. It would make her task so much easier. And she hardly wanted witnesses to the killing. Murder was a solitary business, or ought to be.

Casually she walked amongst the children; those who knew her smiled and welcomed her. She greeted them serenely with no outward manifestation of her design. She was beautifully self-possessed, she was tranquil, she was as usual. But her heart pounded with anticipation. She sat for a time on one of the wooden benches, beside an acquaintance, to relax, to observe. She looked about her, missing nothing.

It was not long before she saw her, her unsuspecting victim and the sight of the small plump figure thrilled her. It would be as she had planned, nothing could go wrong now. But she was in no hurry, her purpose was best achieved deliberately, with caution, with infinite care. She strolled slowly between the roundabouts and swings towards the shelter of the trees. Along the way she stopped to observe the poppies their red and yellow petals fluttering raggedly in the wind, and already she was part of the scenery. She looked back; no one watched her. Swiftly and with ease she disappeared completely into the shrubbery. The children continued to slide down the slides and to swing on the swings while their mothers gossiped. There would be no audience.

She stood, invisible behind the largest tree, her purple shadow flat as a dead leaf and as still. Only her eyes, large and lustful in the small white face, glittered as she watched. Her heart beat steadily, pumping courage into every sinew and muscle. Now she was ready. Her eyes flickered only once as she moved out of the shadows, slowly at first, till with a sudden quick movement she was upon her quarry, brutally squeezing the life from the limp throat, stilling the high-pitched scream almost before it began. immobilised, her victim begged with feeble voice, with final breath, to be spared.

Entirely unaffected, her teeth flashing like rapiers the cat crushed and swallowed the head of the bird. The warm, plump corpse she took gently between her teeth and carried swiftly back to her kittens.

MRS EASTERN

UNTIL SHE had been routed, laid waste to, utterly vanquished, Rose did not realize that war had even been declared. She had no warning and when she finally lost it was altogether too late and quite irrevocable.

"You are so lucky," her friends had said when she became engaged. "You are so lucky. Not only is James the sweetest, most gorgeous man but his mother..." Words would fail. Rose was envied and not only because she had captured the impregnable heart of the adorable James Eastern. His mother, too, was admired universally.

It would be unfair to describe Mrs Eastern as captivating. She was too dignified for that; but she did quite simply captivate everyone. Her behaviour in every possible situation was perfect. She glowed with charm, and the aura surrounding her was one of soothing security. So Rose had no warning whatever. When it came, Mrs Eastern's victory was terrible and complete.

At luncheon parties in Bellevue Hill, in her beautifully-cut silk suits of a colour which suited her complexion, Mrs Eastern smiled and said, "I always hoped that James would marry someone as sweet as Rose. I'm so happy for them."

At afternoon tea in Double Bay she said, "James and I have always been such friends but I know I must let go." She paused and sighed delicately. "I couldn't be happier. Rose is like a daughter to me, the one I never had." And her smile changed from charmingly wistful to gently delighted as she said, "I'm so lucky."

At first Rose mistrusted Mrs Eastern; mistrusted her ease and her at times vague, ingenuous chatter. She mistrusted Mrs Eastern's easy acceptance of James' love for her. A mother letting her son go so lightly did not seem entirely genuine or even right.

At their engagement party in Mrs Eastern's flat overlooking the harbour Mrs Eastern said, while kissing Rose's cheek briefly, "Welcome, my dear. Now that you'll soon be one of the family we'll be able to have lots of lovely chats together." And she smiled secretly at Rose and James, smiled fondly at them both as their friends crowded around wishing them luck and good fortune. Rose felt as though she was in the centre of a charmed circle where nothing could ever harm her, not even Mrs Eastern's secret smile because fleetingly, just for a moment, that smile had frightened her.

Rose and James were married at St Marks, Darling Point, on a steamy summer day. Many people said quietly that this was really an ideal marriage and many smiled enviously as Mrs Eastern threw confetti with all the gusto of a young girl.

After the honeymoon Mrs Eastern left them alone "to settle down", she said to her friends. She did not press for the intimate relationship which Rose had feared. She was friendly but reticent. Rose was relieved and liked her more for her tact. Occasionally she came for dinner and it was fun – the stories she told about her contemporaries were entertaining and often naughty. Sometimes Rose found herself almost shocked but later she realized that, after all, Mrs Eastern was a woman and not merely James' mother. Her life had been fun, her marriage obviously happy. Rose saw that to label Mrs Eastern as sexless, as she had unwittingly done, was ludicrous and quite wrong.

She began to like Mrs Eastern more and more. She began to go to Mrs Eastern's flat for morning coffee. They would sit on the small balcony in the morning sun, watching the movements of the ships and the wind on the water. Their relationship became more intimate and Rose welcomed the intimacy. Mrs Eastern told her about her early life and of her struggles. Her strength in her difficulties was something Rose admired most of all – purposeful strength, which had nearly always got Mrs Eastern what she wanted from life. Rose listened and was disarmed.

Then Mrs Eastern began to tell Rose about James when he was small. It was a new experience for Rose to see James through Mrs Eastern's eyes, in the guise of baby or small boy, and she found it novel and enchanting. Mrs Eastern said, "When he was born I looked after him myself. Everyone had nurses in those days but I wouldn't hear of it. I wouldn't let anyone else touch him. He was much too precious." She laughed fondly at herself.

"After his father died, that was when he was six, I could hardly bear to see him go off to school, I missed him so much. He was everything to me then. And then when he was three... and then when he was five months..."

Mrs Eastern's stories jumped about from age to age and from year to year as though time had not then existed, did not exist now. With Rose's interest to spur her on the stories became more intense. Photographs were found and examined in detail. Each detail had a story; baby James on the beach, in the bath, on his tricycle. Slowly Rose began to tire of baby James.

"Of course I never let him scream," said Mrs Eastern. "I always picked him up." Rose sighed and yawned behind her hand. "And of course he was breast-fed," said Mrs Eastern. Despite herself Rose's eyes crept unwillingly to Mrs Eastern's firm bosom, the bosom where baby James had suckled contentedly, the bosom his tiny hands must have pummelled and stroked. Rose shuddered.

"And I always let him run naked on the beach. He looked so sweet with his little thing bobbing up and down and his little bare bottom so brown and sandy – he did love his freedom." Mrs Eastern's eyes gleamed. "Of course lots of people said I was doing all the wrong things, they criticized me madly; but who was right?" She threw up her hands triumphantly. "Look at James now." Rose looked instead at the capable hands; those hands that had snuggled and cuddled and patted and powdered her James – Mrs Eastern's James. She felt uneasy and cold.

It was after Mrs Eastern had found the baby pictures she had been looking for – those of James naked on the beach, running naked into the water, sitting naked on the sand – and after she had shown them lovingly to an unwilling Rose that James began to find Rose unnaturally silent. She became impatient with him, with his gentleness, with all the things she had loved in him. She began to snap at him for no particular reason and found his forgiveness irritating.

It was one night when James lay naked in the bed beside Rose that his arms reached for her and his hand crept nakedly to her breasts. She responded sleepily; her hand found his bare bottom. Suddenly it became baby James" bare brown, sandy bottom; it was baby James who was briskly, lasciviously stroking, encircling her breast with his naked hand, who was stroking revulsion into her suddenly terrified body. She saw that hand stroking and pushing at Mrs Eastern's bare, firm sensible bosom. She pushed the hand away – far away. "Headache," she whispered, shivering, and baby James, petulantly turning over and away, displayed once again and forever his beautiful bare brown, sandy bottom.

After the divorce Mrs Eastern said, "Such a pity it didn't work out," and nodded kindly to Rose when she saw her in the street.

Anna Remembered

THE BLIND was rattling against the window when Erica awoke. It was the beginning of the storm which had been predicted. She lay quietly, not moving, watching and waiting all alone in the darkness. The blind rattled again, more loudly this time. But she knew it was not the noise of the blind which had disturbed her, it was not the wind beginning to sigh and blow outside, it was something else. Something else had woken her and was here, now, in the house with her. Apprehension made her heart pound as she lay, wrapped tightly in her warm blankets, trying to accustom her eyes to the darkness. To uncover herself and stretch out an arm in order to turn on the light seemed infinitely dangerous so she lay quite still, waiting for the knocking of her heart to subside and listening for the smallest unusual sound. Lying quite rigid she waited, trying to gather her courage, telling herself to relax, to be strong. Telling herself to get up to check the whole house to make sure that all was well. Otherwise she would never get back to sleep, feeling that someone or something was abroad in the night. Abroad in the night; Erica smiled in the darkness at her melodramatic thoughts. What nonsense – she would just turn on the light, put on her gown and go downstairs and there would be nothing there, nothing at all. Then she would go back to her warm bed and laugh at herself and her foolish imaginings. Abroad in the night indeed. She smiled again and yawned a little and then the wind howled. She listened to it, keening like a mourner at a funeral, flying at the windows as though trying to get in, trying to touch her with its anguish. She shivered as she felt a draught on her face like a feather of ice. Why did the wind always howl when Paul was away? Perhaps it was in sympathy with her loneliness, or perhaps she simply did not hear it when Paul was lying close, comforting and warm beside her.

Erica stretched her cramped limbs daringly and then with one quick movement threw the covers back, swung her legs to the floor and bent down to find her slippers. Fearful in the sudden cold, she waited for something to happen but all was still. She switched on the bedside lamp and looked quickly around the room, squinting at the sudden brightness. Again there was nothing. Even the wind seemed quieter now, shut out by the familiar cosy surroundings, despite the utter emptiness of Paul's side of the bed. A little consoled by the warm light, she briskly slipped on her dressing gown, opened the bedroom door and switched on the light in the hall. No one there; cautiously she set off down the stairs.

Again she found nothing, again she saw nothing and heard only the wind still blowing and rapping at the windows and the house still creaking its resistance to the storm.

Erica went first to the kitchen. There she found the milk bottles still on the table, patiently waiting to be put out. She picked them up and went to the back door which to her dismay was unlocked. How casual and forgetful she had been tonight, but then putting out the milk and locking the door were Paul's responsibilities when he was at home. It was easy to forget the bottles but unusual for her not to lock the door – how could she have forgotten that, tonight of all nights, when she was so alone? Uneasily she opened the door and put the milk bottles on the step. The wind was much louder out here and remarkably powerful; it came in strong gusts almost pulling the door out of her hands but with one vigorous push it was shut and then firmly locked.

Erica pushed the hair out of her eyes with her cold hands and wished she were back in her warm bed but there were more rooms to check. She gathered her courage again and with a deep breath opened the sitting-room door and switched on the light. At first everything seemed quite normal but then as her eyes searched anxiously she saw a movement; the thin curtain by the door into the garden billowed hugely as though... as though... but she did not have time to finish the thought. Just as suddenly as they had billowed, the curtains collapsed and there was nothing there at all, only her reflection in the dark glass of the garden door.

It was not relief Erica felt now but fear. With the collapse of the curtains, her courage, so finely gathered, collapsed too and fear, stark cold fear, took over; her whole body was numb with it. Why, oh why was all this happening tonight and why to her? It was almost like a punishment. Was there something she had done, something bad long ago, something wrong? Of course not. Like a child she began to count good and worthy things accomplished and achieved. But, uninvited and unwelcome, Anna stole into her head. Beautiful Anna, even more beautiful perhaps than Erica.

Erica began to sweat, hurriedly she pushed the thought away – that didn't count, had never counted, any of it, none of it. She must go on, check the study and then back to her warm bed, back to safety.

She forced herself to move on, first into the hall, then into the study. Again she found the room empty, normal. As she returned to the hall the wind began to howl again but this time with a far greater intensity as though trying to achieve some impossible feat. At the same moment she heard an earth- shaking crash and with appalling suddenness the lights went out. Erica felt almost extinguished herself;

enclosed all at once in the thick blackness, she felt as though she could hardly breathe. The sweat froze on her body and she began to shiver. This could not be real, this could not be happening to her. It was unfair, she did not deserve such torment. But there was Anna, beautiful Anna, her friend Anna. Weak and trembling now, Erica groped her way slowly to the bottom of the stairs and started upwards. The bannister was cold and sticky under her moist hand but gave her a measure of support, of comfort.

Anna – in the darkness the thoughts rushed again into her unwilling head. Anna – she never saw her now, which was not Erica's fault. Anna should have understood and forgiven like a true friend, not remained implacably silent after accusing Erica of disloyalty; after she discovered the flirtation with Martin – that's all it was really, a harmless flirtation, except an exuberant once or twice. But then that sort of thing happened to everyone, it was not wrong or cheating, it was well, just life, just another experience. It was Anna who was in the wrong, a brief disloyalty was no sin, it was Anna with her unrealistic principles who had started the guilt, this guilt she carried in the dark tonight. It wasn't fair; miserably Erica pulled herself up the stairs, her cold sweaty hands slipping on the bannister with each step. Did everyone remember unpleasant things on nights like this, things pushed away out of sight, events they would rather forget? But why should she forget? Defiantly she remembered, remembered the fun and delight she and Martin had shared; remembered the lies and the deceit, but only for Anna's sake, entirely for Anna's sake, so that she should not be hurt. It was kinder that way – it was how everyone did it, she was not the only one.

Erica struggled on up the stairs justifying herself with every tight breath. What if Paul ever found out? He trusted her, he had always been loyal, always – oh, what did that matter now, he would never find out. Anna, who could have told him, chose to remain silent. But she knew, knew it all very well and had suffered it all; and the rest. Still, it was her own fault, marriages did not break without blame on both sides, it was nothing to do with Erica. And Anna was so beautiful and had always had all the luck; she had survived.

At last Erica reached the top of the stairs. I must stop thinking about all that now, she told herself severely. Guilt is a destructive emotion, a treacherous emotion, I must not let myself be trapped by it any longer, trapped in my thoughts of Anna and those unimportant, far-away events and only because of the dark, because of the wind. I will go back to bed, pull the warm blankets around me and go to sleep and forget this nightmare. At least there was no one in the house, so much was sure.

Erica reached the top of the bannister, the last stair and breathed more easily. Closer to the bedroom now she began to feel a little more calm despite the continuing darkness, and the continuing pounding of her heart. It was only a storm, somewhere power lines had been blown down, cutting off the electricity. Tomorrow, everything would be back to normal.

With infinite relief Erica reached her bedroom. When he came home tomorrow Paul would be so proud of her, proud that she had found the courage to inspect the whole house, to make quite certain that there was no one there, that there was nothing wrong. How silly to have such ridiculous fears.

She sat on the edge of the bed, breathing hard after her ordeal and bent to remove her slippers and then her gown. Tomorrow night Paul would be at home, lying here beside her, holding her warmly in his arms, shutting out fear. The clock on the bedside table glowed and showed her 3. 00 a. m. Thank goodness – it was already nearly morning, not long to wait now.

She slipped into bed. It was just as she pulled the covers more closely around her shoulders that she heard a sound close beside her, a soft chuckle – icy arms and legs entwined with her own, something weighty forced the breath from her body, engulfed her and she recognized at last what it was that had woken her. This untimely knowledge was Erica's last coherent thought as it closed with her.

Overnight the storm blew itself out. The morning was still and clear and there was no wind at all, no breath. Trees stood silent, nothing stirred their leaves. The milk bottles, full now, stood on the step in the sun.

Later in the day, Paul found Erica lying in their tumbled bed on her back, her arms by her side, her hands clenched into fists. Pale and silent she did not see him or hear him, she was unable to speak or move. Her eyes were dreadfully open as though fastened on infinity.

A stroke, the doctor pronounced, unusual but by no means unknown at her age. There was a good chance of almost complete recovery although naturally it would take time.

Strangely, Erica never recovered. But she lived on, unable or unwilling to improve her condition. She did not communicate – perhaps she could not.

Shut away from life she sat alone, staring steadily down the years, shrouded in her mysterious silence.

PLAYING WITH FIRE

ROULETTE IS a game of chance. Look there – see the numbers on the green baize cloth – some are red, some are black, running from number one to number thirty-six, each in its own, small square, its own space. In a rectangle at the top of the cloth, taking up the same space as three whole squares lies the zero. Interesting is it not – the largest space of all reserved for zero – for nought – for nothing. You may bet on that too. You may place your bet on a number or on a colour – on the black or on the red. You may bet on the even numbers or on the uneven numbers. You may bet on many numbers or on one only, guided by intuition, instinct or impulse, on however you see it at that moment, the moment in which you place your chips on the green baize cloth, the moment before the small white ball spins then falls. You may bet or you may watch. To play roulette costs nothing – or everything.

If art imitates life then roulette is art. It not only imitates life, here in this casino set beside the dark waters of the harbour with the opera house a brilliantly-lit beacon in the distance, it is life, for an evening. Here in this the elegant room, gently lit by shimmering, crystal chandeliers, the mirrored walls reflecting the gaming tables, reflecting the exotic, richly-coloured Persian rugs on the polished floor under the stylishly shod feet of the players, fortunes can be made or lost.

See how people play their numbers – watch them. Some play boldly, their faces stern. They place their bets resolutely, then wait, impassively, fatalistically, for the game to begin, for the ball to spin and fall. Others play timidly, uncertainly. See how their minds change, how they move their counters from number to number, from colour to colour, hands hovering over the even numbers column, over the odd numbers column over the red or over the black, intentionally it seems, allowing events to overtake their indecision. They toy with fate, leaving to the very last moment, the moment when the croupier calls "rien ne va plus" and no more bets may be placed, to finally put their chips in place on the table. Still others make no decisions at all. They cast their chips onto the numbered cloth, allowing them to remain where they fall. They are gambling at a distance – fate is entirely out of their hands, luck is all.

Consider the girl sitting there at the roulette table. The pretty one with the shining ash-blonde curls and dark eyes. She has a large stack of counters in front of her. See how confidently she plays the game. Her hands are white, her fingers long and slim. On her wrist she wears a silver bracelet set with a unique harlequin opal – that rare black opal with its red heart of fire, glowing and flashing in the light of the chandelier. Some believe it to be an unlucky stone. What will it bring tonight?

Now see how casually she scatters the chips onto the table and pushes them into place with red- tipped finger nails. She has no fear. She waits – we wait.

The croupier in his black dinner jacket sits before the roulette wheel. With a skilful and practiced flick of his fingers he throws the small white ball into the spinning cauldron of numbers. The ball runs in its appointed direction, the numbers blur as they fly past in the opposite direction until eventually the ball falls into a small square, a numbered, coloured square – perhaps your square, perhaps your number, perhaps your colour if you were able to predict the final resting place of this small, destiny-laden white ball. Call it chance, call it fate or luck, call it what you will. Only one thing is certain, if the ball is cast into the wheel it must come to rest. A number will come up. Some will win, some will lose. That is the charm of the game – its predictability. Some will always win, some will always lose.

Now the ball comes to rest on the red nine and the girl, the pretty girl with the blonde curls has won again. She has won on the red. She is not playing the numbers just now, perhaps she will play them later. She continues to put her chips on the red square as she has been doing all evening – only on the red. As we watch we see that occasionally she does not play. Strangely it is then that a black number comes up. Is it not uncanny – she seems to have the game by the throat. There – she has won again. The croupier pushes the pile of chips towards her – her hands reach out for her winnings. The tower of chips before her is leaning, is threatening to fall it is now so high. She makes two towers, then three, her face thoughtful, intent, waiting for the moment, the right moment to play the red again. But perhaps she will play a number now. Perhaps this time she will place her counters on the black. That is the charm of watching the game – its heart-stopping unpredictability.

Look at the young man sitting opposite, He is entirely engrossed in watching the pretty girl play. It is clear that he has played tonight, played and lost. There are no chips under his hands now and soon he will be obliged to get up from the table, to leave his chair so that someone else may play.

In the meantime, he is watching the game and watching the girl with as much concentration as the girl is watching the white ball fall into its small predestined space. One more spin of the wheel – this time the number is the red twelve and the girl has won again. The young man frowns, what is he thinking as his hands involuntarily close into fists, his knuckles whiten. What is he planning? Now the croupier motions, he must relinquish his seat to another. He moves slowly, he seems reluctant to leave the table but he must. He is a loser. How much could he have lost tonight? From the avaricious expression on his face as he looks at the girl, the girl who is winning, we can assume it has been a big loss.

He goes to the small bar in the comer of the room. He orders a vodka on the rocks and turns again to watch the girl. He sips the clear, icy liquid and sees her put another small stack of counters on the red. The ball is tossed into the spinning wheel, it spins too and spins and spins and finally falls – it comes to rest on the red eighteen. The croupier counts out her winnings and pushes the pile of counters towards her – there are so many they spill onto the cloth in a colourful heap. The girl smiles as she hauls in her winnings with both fine, white hands.

The young man continues to watch, spellbound it seems. See how he admires her, secretly, hiding behind his second vodka. Through the clear ice in the bottom of his glass he sees that the colour of her rich, silk shirt exactly matches the brown velvet of her eyes. As she moves her arms the silk gleams and shines in the glow of the chandelier above her. See how very much he admires her – her beauty, her poise, her style. She is a winner. See too, how he envies her. He puts his glass down and moves towards her table. He is after all, a gambler and although it seems that he lost earlier tonight the evening has not yet ended. For a true gambler and he certainly is one, there is always another challenge, another risk to take, one more chance to tilt at fate.

There now – he is standing behind her chair. He bends down and whispers in her ear.

She looks up, startled. The pearls around her throat glisten, they enhance the whiteness of her neck as she turns to look again. Rapidly she assesses him – the well-fitting light suit, the blue silk tie, the expensive polished shoes. Just as rapidly she makes up her mind.

"Why thank you – I'd love a drink." He smooths back his dark hair, the locks that had fallen over his forehead when he bent down to the girl and asks, "What will it be?" "A vodka martini please." She does not hesitate – she knows what she wants. In his absence she continues to play. She seems completely dedicated to the game.

He returns with her martini and stands behind her chair while she sips and continues to play. Watch her – observe her single-mindedness. She is still winning – always and only on the red. He bends down to speak to her again.

"Why not play a number?" He asks.

"I don't like numbers – there are too many. I like the red."

"Why do you like the red so much – you seem to be absolutely enamoured of the red."

"Red is the colour of fire, of flowers," she turns and looks at him slyly "... of lips."

Does he blush? Perhaps but he hides it well. She is bold, she is a gambler and tonight she cannot lose. He stands behind her chair, he places a hand casually on her shoulder. When she wins he speaks now and again, softly, into her ear. What does he say? We cannot hear because he whispers but we see her smile. Once his fingers caress her neck, her white neck, lightly, almost lovingly. Is she not too trusting of this man, this loser? But between them runs a current, an attraction. Is it the growing tower of chips that lure him or is it the brown velvet of her eyes?

It is late, almost midnight. The girl gathers her counters and prepares to leave. She throws the croupier a chip of high denomination. It is the custom for the winner to tip the croupier, the innocent croupier – innocent of any influence on winner or loser alike. He is merely the instrument in this game. The charm of the game for him is a certain profit – some nights more, some nights less.

The young man helps the girl out of her chair and places a hand under her elbow as she moves towards the teller at the back of the room where she will cash up her winnings. He helps her with her chips. See how friendly, how intimate they have become. A shared intimacy of the sort that often develops between people thrown together at random by circumstances – like victims of a train crash. People who are forced to share a fragment of time in which there is no past and no future, only the totally absorbing present. A situation which monopolises thoughts and minds, which entirely takes over. It is so with roulette – that is the charm of this game of chance.

Let us follow these two gamblers to the end of the evening, to the end of the game. They walk arm in arm. There is rain in the air, see the ring around the moon? A portent some would say. They walk briskly now, her handbag, heavy with money swinging from her shoulder.

"My place?" he asks,

"Why not," she replies. She has the ease, the assurance of a winner. She does not see his smile, fortunately perhaps for it is a mysterious smile, a furtive smile and in the curve of his lips there is an element of triumph. He says,

"I'm so glad you won tonight," his hand on hers, her bag, heavy with money thudding against his body.

"So am I," she replies, her arm cradling her handbag, "I was really very lucky tonight." The bracelet on her arm catches the moonlight – it lights the red vein in the centre of the black gem. Does he see its glitter?

They reach his car, he opens the door for her, settles her. His driving is fast but deft. She likes the way he drives, with certainty, with verve. They sit side by side, not touching but extraordinarily aware of each other. She looks from under her lashes at his face. He looks back at her. He takes his eyes off the road but only for a moment and she sees in them, we see too, a certain anticipation, an expectation – of what? She is unafraid. Brave is she not?

They have arrived. The building is large, new set beside the harbour with views of the bridge.

The lift is beautifully panelled in wood. High above the city he unlocks his door and leads her into a spacious apartment. He draws the curtains and there before them is the moon on the water, the clouded moon. She throws her handbag onto a chair and goes to the window. The harbour is dark with very little traffic at such a late hour. Only a small water taxi, speeding towards Manly makes a trail like a firefly above the waves.

"What a strange night it is," she says, "see the ring around the moon?" She turns and he is not there. She sighs, with apprehension perhaps. But the room is friendly. It is book-lined and comfortable. Nothing bad can happen here, can it?

He returns carrying champagne and glasses on a silver tray. How very well prepared he is. It seems the evening will run its appointed course – the course we all know so well. She at least seems, at the moment, untroubled. Is she gambling again, gambling on a certainty?

He uncorks the lightly-frosted bottle – there is a satisfactory sigh and he pours the bubbling champagne into each glass. He takes the glasses to the window and hands one to her.

"Well...?" The question hangs between them. Slowly she raises her glass to him,

"I think I'll say... good luck..." she smiles and sips. Does she tremble, is she at last, hesitant?

"I'll drink to that" he says "but it's a bit too late - I needed all that luck tonight."

He laughs as he drinks and looks into her eyes.

"But then my luck could change, could it not?" he glances meaningfully at her heavy handbag. She follows his eyes sharply,

"It's mine – all mine."

"Of course it is," he says softly and slides his arm around her waist.

"But come, look at the moon, see how it shines on the water." If she was momentarily afraid she is so no longer. The softness of his voice is reassuring, is seductive. They stand comfortably together, sipping champagne and watching the waves darken then lighten to silver as the clouds scud across the face of the moon. She is quite relaxed now, she leans against him. After a time they turn away from the moon and their lips meet, their lips touch. It is a gentle kiss. It is inevitable. Gently he takes the glass from her hand and kisses her again. She responds, gladly, willingly, and her fingers caress the back of his neck. His arms are around her. He looks into her eyes as though all life's secrets will be revealed in their depths – the secrets of love, the secret that makes her a winner. Love – a gamble is it not? The length and breadth of it as unpredictable as the infinite colours of the sea – yet the fact of its imperishable existence as predictable as the rising of the moon.

He leads her to the sofa – his grasp is firm. In an instant, quite suddenly he takes her right arm and bends it smoothly behind her back. Startled, she cries out. He has taken her completely by surprise, there was no, warning, or did she disregard the signs? She straggles wildly, hopelessly. He is the stronger. She is utterly helpless – imprisoned against the cushions. He smiles down at her and motions towards the handbag, the bag, heavy with money lying on the chair.

"And now it's mine – all mine." His voice has a new authority, his mouth, a moment ago so tender, is set.

With her eyes she pleads for release. He does not soften, he is determined, he is pitiless. Brave still, outraged to be caught thus, to be tricked so easily she cries angrily,

"You wouldn't dare..." But he is relentless.

"I dare... and more..." he tells her. She is limp now, in his grasp. What will she do, what can she do? Did she not gamble on the red tonight, on the red of his lips, on the red that has finally failed to come up.

"Please let me go... please" she looks deep into his eyes to move him with her own.

"Please... please..." she begs again, she must beg, that is all that is left for her now, only entreaty. He becomes even more callous.

"No..." We ache with her, we feel her anger, her fear, her fury, her frustration. Now his free hand encircles her neck, her soft, white neck. Is this her destiny?

"You'll never get away with it" she says. It is a final, futile act of bravado.

"I won't...?"

"No... I'll... I'll..." she struggles again, breathlessly.

But it is useless. She knows in her heart that the game is over.

His hand leaves her throat and goes to his pocket. What has he got there – a gun – a knife? Slowly his hand emerges, something glitters, something flashes. He brings it slowly, deliberately to the level of her eyes. He lets her look long at what he has there. It is torture for her – for us. What is it he has in his hand?

And then we see that it is not a knife, it is not a gun, it is a small, silver box. It springs open to reveal a ring, a ring set with a harlequin opal that flashes with its inner fire of deep, glowing red, a red that matches the fire of her bracelet.

"Happy anniversary my darling, my lovely, my beautiful winner" he says, victorious now and covers her lips with his own.

FLEUR

HE WAS a truly happily married man. An honourable man. A man who had no intention, indeed no need to seek new amatory experiences or new sexual partners. His busy life left him no time to speculate on matters of that sort. His wife, his beautiful, bountiful Fleur, entirely satisfying in every way, was all he had ever needed, was all he would ever need.

To be in a strange Asian city on business, as he was now, was nothing new for him. He had been here before, had rejected before his host's offers of slim, sloe-eyed young ladies who came to dine and giggled generously, who placed cool, experienced hands on his thighs under the table, who hinted boldly and whispered softly. He had rejected them with the aplomb and self-confidence of a man completely secure in his masculinity, in his virility. And had dismissed too, with equanimity, any sly imputations of his prudery. Tonight would be no different. He had accepted his host's suggestion of a bathe and massage before dinner without demur. The long flight had tired him, a massage would soothe, would relax him. And a massage was all it would be, there was no need to go further, he would not go further. He laughed off easily his host's veiled implications and spoke deliberately of Fleur at home, his Fleur whom he loved without qualification, unconditionally, completely.

Their destination was a little way out of town, his host explained. The chauffeur-driven limousine was supplied with a cocktail cabinet and even boasted fresh ice. The Scotch was good and gradually he began to unwind from the strain of the long flight. Soon they arrived at a large villa, set in extensive gardens, well hidden from the road. This establishment was clearly elegant and expensive and new to him. His host told him that it had only recently opened and was especially exclusive and luxurious.

They entered and were welcomed effusively by many smiling, cunningly half-dressed young girls, all very beautiful, all labelled above their hearts with a name – Suzie, Dolly, Candy or Jayne. It was explained that he must choose one, she would see to all his needs. He chose, he thought, at random, one who hung back a little, whose long hair fell forward hiding her breasts. Perhaps she seemed more anonymous than the others. She was dark and her hair was black. Fleur was fair with short blonde curls – but what had that to do with it? He dismissed the thought.

He noted, as she took him by the hand, that she was short and slim, as too was Fleur. Her perfume, as she led him to a changing room, clung sweetly, rather too sweetly he thought. Thankfully and quickly he removed his crumpled clothes and entered the main room. It was small but well-proportioned and contained a round, black-tiled bath which was steaming faintly as the girl let hot water in. On small tables there were low, pink lights which cast round, deep shadows. On one of them stood a vase containing sprays of orchids in shades of cream, red and purple. To one side a mattress, large and firm, simply draped with pink sheets. Beyond it, pink curtains hung to the floor, while the far mirrored wall reflected and doubled the whole. A curiously cool, pink, innocent glow suffused the room. He breathed deeply of the mingling perfumes and sank gratefully into the bath.

The girl began to speak – to chat. She was not difficult to talk to, but then she was trained for that. Was his flight tiring? Would he like a cocktail? Champagne perhaps? Yes, champagne, why not, he deserved it after his tiring journey. She brought it in a long thin glass. He sipped gladly – it was a good year. Silently he saluted his host, at least this was being done with flair, with style. But was there an element of seduction; were his host's endeavours aimed at seeing him finally yield to the temptations of more ordinary men? Now soft hands began to soap him, gently across the shoulders, across his chest, slowly down the length of his arms, hands like silk. He let his head fall back and closed his eyes. The feeling was delightful and infinitely relaxing. He could feel the tension easing, sliding away, even as her hands slid smoothly, wetly across his chest, under his arms and down. He looked up and saw the whole scene reflected in the mirrored wall, saw himself being soaped, almost caressed and realized again that the girl was very beautiful. Her long black hair falling forward as she bent over him had a sheen and the profile it revealed was strikingly lovely. But not like Fleur, not nearly as beautiful as Fleur. He closed his eyes again. The sensations went on.

He and Fleur had often discussed infidelity, seriously and, as they discussed most things, honestly.

"I don't mind what you do," she always said. "You are a free man, I want you to know that. I never want the thought of me to hold you back from any new experience you feel you must have. You may be tempted, I suppose inevitably you will be. But then if you deny yourself you may blame me – you may love me less. I don't want that. So please, never tell me, promise me you will never tell me. If I ever found out I don't think I could bear it. I don't know what I would do – perhaps I would have to retaliate, do the same to you." Her eyes held his and he could see the pain beneath the bravado. Was she really giving him freedom or merely the illusion of freedom? He knew that if he gave in to a fleeting temptation, no matter how meaningless for him, Fleur would guess. Their relationship was too close. It would be a betrayal and something would be lost, be ended and irrevocable. No matter how sensible, how intelligent, how open and honest their relationship, it would fall apart. And at what cost – a cheap, quick thrill.

He shook off the silky hands and held out his glass for more champagne. The bubbles rose – but why was he thinking in this morbid, serious vein. Relax and enjoy this, he told himself, nothing more will happen. In any case Fleur would never know any of it, not even this innocent bath. There was no need whatever to tell her. And he could resist this child's blandishments; she was indeed little more than a child he now saw, looking at her properly for the first time. He saw, through the brief transparent chiffon wrap, tied only at the neck and designed to fall fully open, a firm young body – except for the breasts, so rounded and full and set superlatively high above the tiny waist. Her whole body was an even shade of *cafe au lait,* and as creamy – it cried out to be touched. He looked away.

She held out a large pink towel and invited him to lie down on the mattress. When he stepped out of the bath she wrapped him in the towel and patted him dry. He accepted her care with composure, as though he was used to being pampered like this every day, as though it was his due. Then he lay face down on the cool pink sheets. He felt comfortable and warm and loose in every joint. He felt as light as air. The girl poured something aromatic onto her hands and began to massage him. She stroked him with a slow, gentle, even rhythm. The perfume from the sweet spicy oil rose from his warm body and filled the room. More quickly now she rubbed the pungent oil smoothly down the length of each leg, one after the other, up and down, up and down. He closed his eyes and gave himself up to the sharpness of the feeling. Expertly she kneaded and stroked and rubbed, making him aware of every muscle in every separate part of his body, making all of his skin tingle and smart, compelling his whole body to respond to her. Softly she began to whisper in his ear, words and phrases no child ever knew. She leant closer as she whispered and like a small bird bit gently and repeatedly, his ear, his neck, his shoulder and he shivered with the intensity of the pleasure. He felt her breasts whisper across his back as she went on stroking strongly, smoothly dissolving the last threads of resistance. He forgot tomorrow – there was only now; and now he would let himself fall, would sink, would plunge into these unbearably exquisite sensations.

He turned over and opened his arms to her. She came into them with a smile as he in his turn began to caress her. There was only one thought now, that of fulfillment, of pleasure so intense he was already breathless with the anticipation of it. And he would have it. Roughly he grasped her, quickly he turned her to lie beneath him. He bent towards her mouth and as suddenly stopped. His hands fell numbly away from her body and the breath caught in his throat as though it had been switched off. He could not breathe. The girl's long black hair had fallen across the pinkness of the sheet, and through the transparent wrap he saw her superb shoulders and breasts. She lay looking up at him expectantly but there, embroidered on the chiffon, just above one of her deliciously firm, deliciously full, invitingly pink-tipped breasts, now forever unattainable, he read the name 'Fleur'.

THE SUNGLASSES

IT WAS Clare's first party without him. She stood alone at the top of the stairs waiting uneasily for her guests, feeling the same cold emptiness that had been there, filling her, ever since Alec had left her. He had left her for an artful pretty girl with sharp brown eyes and ambitions. A friendly open girl. Clare had liked her and her tenacity in striving to overcome a poor and stagnant background; had liked her and had been easily and ridiculously deceived by her. The enormity of the trite situation fell upon her again, suffocatingly, and she flushed with shame as her first guests came with pity in their eyes to kiss her. Poor Clare, how pale she looked, how cruelly she had been used. They brought her flowers and bottles of wine and their company to soothe the hurt. They fussed and petted and kissed her and were much too kind. Clare accepted their ministrations lifelessly – nothing really helped.

But soon the music began and then they were all there, filling the house with reassuring laughter. Clare passed the strawberry punch and smiled too but it was as though from a distance; from the vacuum of Alec's absence which was still like a transparent wall around her. In it she was alone. She smiled and laughed but felt as though she was waiting. Much later she remembered that she had indeed been waiting; waiting and aching to feel normal again, longing to lose that queer sense of being separate. Together the couples moved and danced, and chattered and laughed. Alone Clare smiled and handed around punch.

By the open window a breeze stirred the daisies in the terra cotta vase and then Clare saw them. The sunglasses, strange sunglasses lay on the window sill, forgotten. They lay quietly, like a small brown animal – like a shiny poisonous animal because Clare with sudden revulsion recognized them. How often she had seen them on that sharp little face – Dior, and brown like her eyes. How proud she had been of them too. So Alec had brought the girl to this house, to Clare's and Alec's house after all. Despite all his promises and assurances. She had been here, and with him. Clare felt weak. Apprehensive, too, as though something awful was about to happen. But of course it had already happened and there they were, the sunglasses, brown and shiny like her eyes, piercing Clare all over again. Not with pain this time but with an increasing overwhelming anger. That Alec, with his so-called sensitivity – with his almost aggressive sensitivity – could achieve something so finally squalid was monstrous. But at the same time it was a strange kind of relief to feel such fury. Here it was, the final proof of his unforgivable and indecent indifference to the past and to their love. It was as though he had deliberately killed something. Perhaps now some of the pain and regret of his loss could be written off against this consummate outrage.

Furiously Clare sipped her punch. Its icy sweetness cooled her hot cheeks a little. Then mistily, through the frosted glass, she could see a shape coming towards her. It was Roger, his arms stretched wide.

"Dance?" he said, and then, "but Clare what is it, what's the matter?" He put his arms around her. She was pale now and her eyes shone with contempt.

"It's Alec," said Clare violently. "He's had her in this house – in our house." She glanced at the window sill where the sunglasses lay, menacingly it still seemed, and watching.

"They're hers?" asked Roger. Clare nodded. He put out his hand to take them and Clare flinched as though she thought they might bite. Roger put them on, hooking the arms carefully behind his ears, and before Clare could protest steered her onto the verandah towards the music.

With his arms tight around her, from behind the dark lenses he murmured comfort as they danced, and gradually Clare relaxed.

"How do I look?"

The glasses were sliding slowly down Roger's nose. Behind the elegant frames he looked comical and kind and his arms around her were warm. Clare began to feel better. Roger pushed the sunglasses back onto his nose, pushed hard to force them on more securely and they both heard the crack as one of the arms gave way.

"Careful," said Clare lightly and then watched, fascinated, as the glasses began to slide down again, faster this time because of the loose arm. Roger lifted his chin to stop them. They danced faster and the glasses slid further.

"Oh dear," said Roger, to the ceiling, "what if they should fall?"

"What if, indeed," Clare pushed purposely against him and laughed aloud as the glasses shook and slid and fell with a tinkle to the floor. One of the lenses cracked.

Moving with the music Clare kicked the glasses lightly away, across the verandah.

Roger following, kicked them back. The cracked lens fell out. The one in which Clare had seen a shadowy figure with brown eyes moving, purposefully it seemed, towards her, as though to strike her, or to stop her.

"What a pity," said Clare, treading on it. Glass and eyes crunched under her foot.

"Pity," said Roger dancing Clare over the glass, sending splinters flying. They danced faster, kicking the sunglasses backwards and forwards across the verandah, in time to their dancing and to the music. Their faces became more serious as they concentrated. Roger trod delicately and the cracked arm snapped as it came off. He trod on it again and ground it hard into the floor. They swayed together over the glasses, more slowly now, kicking gently, inflicting damage more deliberately. When the other lens fell out Clare spun round on it savagely, her dark hair flying.

"Poor eyes, all gone now," she said, spinning.

Those brown shiny eyes that had looked at Clare, honestly, not like the ones who tell you lies with shifting eyes, a straight look as she had said, "Yes, Clare, do cut your hair, short all over, it will look gorgeous."

"Roger did you like my hair short?"

"No it didn't suit you at all."

Clare stamped pitilessly. Her face was flushed and eager. Glass covered the whole verandah and they scattered splinters with each purposeful step. On and on they danced, clutching each other tightly, absorbed and breathless with effort, intent on reducing what remained of the awful brown thing to dust, to nothing. The crushing, grinding, and tinkling sounds made a strange accompaniment to the slow primitive ritual and finally to their kiss which was like the fierce fulfillment of a ceremony, of a murder. some days later Alec rang, diffident but shameless, asking for the sunglasses. How honest, and how impervious he is, has always been, thought Clare indifferently, and this time felt no pang at the sound of his voice. He began to explain in long and plausible detail how he had come to be in the house – "But Alec," interrupted Clare. And then with immense serenity and feeling lighter, as though set free from an enforced period of mourning, she said, "But Alec there are no sunglasses in this house, no sunglasses at all."

CELEBRATION FOR MONICA

TODAY IS my fortieth birthday. I have been comforted by my husband – a long golden chain; by my children – sticky consoling kisses, chocolate rum truffles (my favourites) and a rainbow silk scarf. Here are the compensations of the inevitable. The more durable gifts will mark the event in my mind forever – in case I should sometimes forget.

Now I am sitting in the garden reading the paper and listening to the birds. My fortieth birthday – the thought is still a surprise, there has been no time yet to become accustomed to it. But it is spring, as it always is on my birthday and that delicious expectant smell of summer is already in the air. I still feel its promise despite the enormity of the milestone achieved today, so effortlessly it seems; that is the real surprise, and so much sooner than I expected.

The sun is shining, my roses gently drop their pink and white petals on the grass and I turn the pages of the newspaper aimlessly – hardly reading, merely glancing – until a picture catches my eye. A large house set behind ornate and massive wrought iron gates, a glimpse through them to a lovely garden with huge old trees. Inset is a smaller picture of a face, a woman, shadowy and indistinct but I recognize her at once. The faint smile, the steadfast eyes – it is the older but still flawless face of Monica Hewett. So this was her destiny, behind those expensive gates. I am not at all surprised, it was only to be expected – she was always lucky.

Monica Hewett and I shared a school, a class and almost a birthday (ours were a week apart) for five years. Monica Hewett – her mellifluous name still flows in my mind with the same undercurrent of glamour which she entirely embodied over all those years. Monica Hewett, the most beautiful girl in our class, the one we envied, the one we all secretly wished we could be. She had light apricot-blonde hair, naturally curly, brown velvet eyes and every summer her skin turned golden brown all over. While we fought to put our lily-white legs in every available ray of sunshine, Monica sat in the shade. While our constant struggle for an even tan often resulted in red or blistered patchwork quilt effects, Monica never even had a strap mark. In winter she retained an even dusting of fawn, she did not become slug-like, like us. She was clever, she rarely failed exams and to top it all she was nice. Not smug, not bitchy, not patronizing, as she easily could have been; not superior in any way. We all liked her, she was one of us. Except that to us her future seemed magically assured, ours quite uncertain.

We were fifteen when the dancing classes began. They were held in the local Town Hall after school and attended, in school uniform by those boys and girls who were interested in familiarizing themselves with the foxtrot, the waltz or the opposite sex. In our case it was mainly boys, a subject we knew little or nothing about. Thus, on dancing days we apprehensively polished our shoes as carefully as our faces, put our school hats as far back on our heads as gravity would allow and pretended to each other that we would enjoy ourselves.

The weekly dancing class was governed by formal though unwritten rules of behaviour. While we talked about boys, though not very seriously, we certainly did not speak to them nor they to us. The afternoon always began with everyone sitting around the sides of the hall in rows like half-grown flowers, boys on one side girls on the other, waiting for Mrs Meggitt, who played the piano and instructed, to begin. Mrs Meggitt (popularly known as old Maggot) was, we thought, very old and particularly ugly. She always wore a strange furry hat over what we took to be a faded blonde wig and long old-fashioned silk frocks in violent colours which never matched her heavily applied lipstick.

Mrs Meggitt, who was probably not as stupid as we supposed, always started with a Barn Dance. This required the girls to form a circle in the middle of the hall and the boys another circle around them. Thus, partners did not need to be chosen, they were simply there and no speaking was necessary – a boon to each bashful breast. When the music began, off we went, changing partners as demanded by the dance and Mrs Meggitt who shouted instructions in a loud sharp voice over her pounding of the piano. At the end of the Barn Dance everyone was left with a partner and the more serious instruction began. The foxtrot – slow, slow, quick, quick, slow – or the waltz, always a disaster. We slid about the floor gingerly as though on board ship in a mid-ocean swell. Couples held each other warily, as one holds an injured bird, ready for anything and particularly for the moment when the music would stop. God forbid that anyone was seen to be dancing too closely or to hold hands a second too long. As soon as Mrs Meggitt stopped playing couples sprang apart as though surprised by torchlight in flagrante delicto.

As the afternoon wore on, palms became sweaty, concentration waned and Mrs Meggitt called half-time. Again, we took up places on opposite sides of the room, again casting only surreptitious glances at our partners on the other side. We did have favourite boys at the class but more from a sense of duty than from genuine interest. It was fun to pick out one and pronounce him rather handsome but that was as far as it went – merely window shopping. We gave them nicknames (since we did not speak we did not know their names); the Teddy bear – he looked plump and cuddly; Ape – he had strangely long arms; and Dimples – for obvious reasons. Dimples clearly liked Monica, he could occasionally be seen to stare at her rather longer than was necessary and on the rare occasions when boys were required to choose a partner (Mrs Meggitt insisted that every aspect of dancing be correctly learnt), Dimples chose Monica twice out of four times. Significant indeed in the days when nonchalance was all and one could not possibly admit to a serious interest in the opposite sex.

However, during the ten minute break, while we all sat in rows to catch our breath, there were one or two of the older girls who went outside with some of the older boys – to smoke, it was whispered. We thought them very audacious and envied their ability to meet the boys' stares as boldly as they did. It was rumoured, too, that they let boys touch them with more than their eyes. One day after class it was one of these girls who told us that Sam Brook, the undoubted dashing hero of the dancing – just seventeen and a James Dean look-alike – had stated that Monica Hewett looked better in school uniform than any other girl he'd ever seen. Praise indeed and true. We were more impressed by this observation than Monica who was flattered by Sam's admiration but not unduly. Compliments of that kind had become her natural due. But she accepted them so modestly and matter-of-factly that we never minded and by now we were becoming used to them too.

On looking back now, I think it was this remark of Sam's coupled with a further discussion about Mrs Meggitt the next day which set Monica off.

We were sitting on the grass under the pepper tree eating our sandwiches, white legs in the sun in rows, discussing Mrs Meggitt's hat. Undoubtedly rabbit, we had finally decided, when Monica unleashed a sudden and uncharacteristic attack on the poor woman.

"Mrs Meggitt is the ugliest person I have ever seen," Monica said violently. "She is so ugly I can't bear to look at her, I wonder how anyone can bear to look at her." The thought offended her terribly we could see.

"Poor old Maggot – she's not as bad as all that," someone said.

"She is, she is," repeated Monica. And then passionately, "People as ugly as that shouldn't be alive at all."

Someone else said, "But she's just old..."

"Old, old, old" interrupted Monica. "How horrible to be old, I can't bear the thought. When I turn forty I will kill myself."

This last statement was made quietly but we were more startled by it than by her former vehemence. Mainly because she sounded as though she meant it.

"Don't be silly," I said, "you'd never do it."

"I will," said Monica with conviction. "I've thought about it quite often and that's what I've decided to do."

"But why?" we asked.

"Because then I'll be ugly and I don't want anyone to see me like that."

We understood that. We all agreed that we'd certainly be ugly at forty although it was generally unthinkable that one would ever be forty. I think we imagined, if we thought about it at all, that on our (mythical) fortieth birthday, the face and body would suddenly fall apart, somewhat like Dorian Gray. Our imaginations then did not encompass slow decay. So Monica's statement was not questioned on those tenuous grounds. Neither did we think to ask her how she would kill herself, the question did not even occur to us. We understood that Monica's outburst was purely the declaration of a philosophy, unencumbered by practicalities. A courageous philosophy. Secretly we admired her romantic resolve although we did remonstrate. The future was ahead, alive with possibilities and here was Monica speaking already and in such a composed manner, of death.

"You won't do it – you'll change your mind."

"I will," repeated Monica serenely. "I will do it. When I turn forty I will kill myself."

It was the way she said it, so utterly convincing, so utterly convinced herself, that made us realize that here was something she had thought about often and at some length.

Trying to make light of it, someone else said, "But anyway its millions of days till you're forty."

"It's only twenty-four years," said Monica matter-of-factly. We digested this measurement – it still felt light years away. "You're fifteen now," said Monica, "and you can remember when you were three or four can't you? Well, that was only twelve years ago and twenty-four is only double that, isn't it?" It was indeed. Forty suddenly loomed over the horizon. Like the rising sun, it became a real possibility. We thought about it a moment more and all at once our sandwiches tasted like straw.

"But there's tons of time between now and then, simply tons," someone else said rather desperately.

"It might go more quickly than you think," said Monica portentously.

And now here I sit in my spring garden and it's gone, all that endless time we seemed to have up our sleeves; vanished as surely as a magician's pack of cards thrown carelessly into the air. Monica was right, those boundless years were used up much more quickly than any of us had been able to believe. But I don't feel old and ugly, I don't even feel forty and I can't imagine Monica ever being ugly, even at eighty. She couldn't have become old and ugly any more than I am old and ugly but we are both undeniably forty.

I read the paragraph in the paper again. Again, it tells me that yesterday the wife of the owner of this house (pictured above) was found dead after a party, floating in the swimming pool. An accident – there were no suspicious circumstances said the police. Was it her birthday party? Was it an accident? It could have been, though the "how" hardly matters now. I look at the shadowy picture again but I see Monica more clearly in Dimples" arms – cool, composed and beautiful in her school uniform, and fifteen years old. I feel fifteen again and once again I find I envy Monica Hewett. I envy her courage and I envy her victory – but then she was always lucky.

A sudden wind ruffles the roses and I fold the paper in half and hurry indoors to prepare for my birthday dinner. I will drink a toast tonight, a toast to Monica Hewett – forever beautiful, forever only forty.

VICTIM

WHERE IS she now – Edie – (pronounced Eedie – short for Erica) poor little Edie? I hear she haunts the halls of group therapists, psychotherapists and distress counsellors of all kinds who deal with a variety of psychological disturbances and where they call her Erica – a name unsuited to her person. When we were children Edie was an ideal name for her; for Edie was a natural – a natural victim. Whenever I hear of yet another rape and someone says "she asked for it" I think of Edie.

I can still see her – the large round face with its flat koala bear nose, red apple cheeks, the big, wet, ingenuous eyes – a solemn face. She was one and a bit years younger than we were – nine to our sophisticated double figures ten nearly eleven, but she seemed even younger than that. She followed us around like a frolicsome puppy, wanting to play, eager to join in all our activities, keen to fetch and carry (her only and infrequent advantage) everlastingly trying to please. But Edie was a pest, just like a too- demanding puppy, even to the pink tongue-tip showing between her teeth because of course Edie had a lisp too, an unattractive lisp. A further aggravation.

It was not only her misunderstanding of our fine sense of humour that irritated us – that she did not laugh at the incomprehensible behaviour of the grown-ups as we did – that she did not pour scorn on their weird habits as we did. Unlike us she respected authority, provoking our contempt, relied on it and yet (a harbinger of her ultimate fate?) was often disappointed.

We were all, the four of us, only children and were thrown together quite often since our parents shared many interests all of which bored us but seemed to consume them. Only children we were – spoilt we were not; not exactly ignored – but overlooked, necessarily brought along too – accessories, like handbags. If not bushwalking, which we loathed, it was an invitation to lunch or high tea with classical music and much serious unintelligible conversation. We were urged to make no noise while the precious, easily breakable phonograph records were placed on turntables where music was forced from them with resharpened fibre needles. This delicate and serious operation was for adults only. The children were put out like cats. Our parents assumed we would play together, indeed ordered us to do so and demanded that we leave them strictly alone. So when Edie told on us, which she did frequently, it was often to no avail. When their music played they became deaf to any intrusion. Had we cried "Fire" they probably would not have heard. "stay outside and play" was the order.

But none of us wanted to play with Edie because playing was not something she understood. Solemnly she watched us, earnestly she tried to do whatever we were doing, desperately she tried to copy us but she was always either physically or mentally unable to do so. She was terribly consistent in her clumsiness of action and of thought. Her conversation too, was not only babyish but predictable. It consisted of endless questions as to why we did whatever we were doing; why we said what we said; why we thought as we did. She never understood our exasperated answers. As a companion she was a liability as well as insufferable. Was she merely stupid? Occasionally we thought so but that explanation did not satisfy us. We had heard her parents boasting of her success at school – first in the class no less which made her a swot – an added annoyance. Sometimes we conjectured that it was her age but dismissed that too as a reason for her behaviour and our antipathy. When necessary, we played quite happily with other, younger children. Edie we all decided, was unique and someone we would dearly love to have seen bound, gagged and thrown into a well.

There was the time we went to the creek at the bottom of our garden to catch tadpoles. We took off our shoes and socks and paddled quietly in the shallow pools where the swift little creatures lurked. Hands were cupped together to make a kind of net and when a tadpole swam into the pale palms, the hands were quickly closed and the slimy little pre-frog popped into the glass jars we had brought with us. Edie was the only one who could not catch a tadpole no matter how hard she tried. 'show me how, show me how" was the constant provoking wail as she splashed clumsily about in the water, stirring up mud and weeds and making our own fishing more difficult. Naturally she was the one who eventually slipped on a mossy stone and fell into the creek. Her pretty dress was soaked and of course she had a wet bottom which caused tears and which, being entirely used to Edie's bawling, we ignored. It was our constant endeavour to ignore her but how does one ignore a big wailing lump like Edie. She was always there – behind us, stuck like a shadow to our enterprises, always in the way.

It says much for our endurance that we did not push her into the creek ourselves but we were already too circumspect to use actual physical violence on Edie. We had long ago learnt that any assault on the person of Edie was impractical – sorely tempted though we were. We knew that this manner of ridding ourselves of her eternal mealy-mouthed sycophancy was one that would not be tolerated by the authorities. In this particular instance we had a simple but effective recourse. When we returned with three tadpoles in a jar, three being all we were able to catch in the muddied water, Edie in her wet frock ran crying to the grown-ups -

"They won't let me share their tadpoles – they are so mean – they won't let me share their tadpoles." The tears ran down her big flat face and our parents merely laughed, retelling the story later as something rather cute. Poor misunderstood Edie; the seeds of her status as victim were already being established and flourished on such unlikely foundations.

From this experience alone we felt she should have learnt to curtail at least her talebearing but Edie was not one to learn from experience. She continued to blubber and snivel and inform officialdom of our transgressions and instead of our acceptance and approval which she dearly sought, earned only our further contempt. And, truly victim-like, she seemed to lose not only our respect but also the support of the grownups.

When luncheon parties were in progress the children were often placed at a table in another room – a system very much to our liking. The further away from the eyes and ears of our parents the better. But the fly in that particular ointment was the inevitable and unwelcome (to put it mildly) presence of Edie. Unable to use physical means to shut her up we were forced to use psychological warfare – a system much in use by our schoolmasters and mistresses – lessons we learnt easily and reproduced with expertise. We would tell jokes – of the puerile kind that even Edie could understand. We saw it as a challenge to outdo each other in the telling of them and would egg each other on to sillier and ever more foolish stories. Soon she would be laughing and it was usually not long before she would beg us to stop making her laugh so that she could eat her lunch. She might as well have double-dared us. Before very long with tears of laughter and by now, chagrin pouring down her face Edie would proceed to the adults" table – irritatingly interrupting their conversation.

"They won't stop making me laugh – they won't stop making me laugh" she howled. In their turn our elders merely laughed and told her to go away and eat her lunch. Poor, poor Edie. I wonder now about her own mother and father and their seemingly careless and unsupportive attitude. Did this encourage Edie's behaviour, drive her on? Since she was an only child and as there was clearly no evidence of bodily harm accompanying her complaints, her parents may have felt it was all simply a part of growing up and of learning to play with other children, that it was good for her developing psyche. Perhaps they felt that Edie would have to make her own way in the world and that these small incidents were all part of learning how to deal with the inevitable vicissitudes of life. On the other hand perhaps, she was the same Edie at home and perhaps her parents were fed up with her and were only too glad to be rid of her if only for an afternoon. Certainly, her behaviour was consistently frightful. Was she not the only child at a birthday party who had burst into tears at the laden festive table and cried uncontrollably. When asked the reason for her outburst she had indicated the delicious spread and sobbed,

"I can't eat any more but I want to – I want to, but I can't!" The laughter at Edie's expense, was universal.

There is only one incident in the sad history of Edie that I sometimes remember with disquiet.

We were playing at a friend's house, Beethoven issued forth into the garden at enormous decibels and we were bored. We had run out of games and talk and Edie as usual was at her worst – constantly asking questions and when given answers whining a tedious and monotonous "why" like any tiresome four-year old. Then someone noticed a small gate in the lattice surrounding the base of the house – an entry to the underneath, the cellar of the house. We decided to explore and, limpet-like, Edie followed. The catch on the gate was rusty but after some pushing, gave way. Slowly we entered a dark world of cobwebs, dirt and dust. On the ground lay old bits of wood and higgledy-piggledy piles of bricks which we knew if touched or moved would expel large black and dangerous spiders. We ventured further into the unknown, accosted by huge dark shapes, probably packing cases or old suitcases and after more stumbling finally reached a wall. There seemed to be nothing worth our further investigation and as we turned to leave someone screamed – she had run into a cobweb. Impelled by thoughts of more spiders crawling over our faces we ran for the gate. Edie following, tripped over a brick and was left a long way behind. Out in the sunshine we only had to look at one another to agree. The opportunity was irresistible. Together we pushed the gate shut and fastened the rusty catch. And then we ran as though the devil himself was in pursuit. We did not wish to hear Edie's screams for we had no doubt that she would bellow as never before. We ran around to the other side of the house where we stopped to catch our breath. We congratulated each other on the bold move for bold and even foolhardy it certainly was. We kicked stones for a time and then gradually became guiltily silent. We listened, we strained to hear something, anything. Only the distant scratchy sounds of a string quartet floated on the still air. Apprehension gripped us – had she died of fright? Anything was possible with Edie. As one we ran back to the scene of our crime – for crime it had suddenly become. Murder no less.

Edie stood at the lattice gate, silent, tears dried in dirty tracks. on her flat face. A face which, surprisingly, had acquired a kind of grubby dignity. She said nothing as she was released from her prison and all at once as well as relief at seeing her living, breathing presence we felt ashamed of our shabby trick. She emerged slowly, majestically and we watched her, almost with a kind of admiration. Once well past us, Edie broke into a run, back towards the music and authority. Her loud sobbing was audible all the way into the depths of the house. The moment was over, the transformation of Edie reversed. We laughed, our unease lifted, everything was back to normal.

Edie was a victim, a victim of her own conduct, of her own character. I feel no guilt because of her subsequent failures in life – and there were to be many. She was forced upon us by circumstances and though we did our best to ignore her, her mere presence made it impossible for us to do so. And yet fundamentally we behaved without malice. Somehow, we felt driven to tease her, to treat her as we did. She was already a victim then, when we were children and she continued to be one.

Victims like Edie are simply born; or are they made by circumstances, by life or some might even say by other people?

THE WAKE

THEY HAD just come back from burying him. His mother's dog welcomed them at the door with sharp, shrill yelps of joy. He jumped and sprang and nipped indiscriminately, ecstatic at their return. Offered such a convenient excuse, they were at last able to smile. They smiled as they bent to pat him, exclaimed at his exuberance and stretched with secret relief. The service – sombre, impersonal but at the same time unctuously sentimental – had made them feel, as these affairs often do, guilty. They were alive, he was dead, and so terribly young.

The mourners too were young, as he had been, and unaccustomed to funerals; such ceremonies were still far removed from their experience. They continued to bend down and pat the small jumping shape, gathering courage for the next step in the ritual. Most of them would later remember this day as a milestone, their first funeral; an uneasy milestone in any life.

His mother showed them into her sitting room. The dog, a small brown spaniel with bulging eyes and a snub nose, led the way triumphantly, his long ears bouncing with every joyful movement, as carefree as though chasing butterflies. The room was ready for the occasion, tables bearing pale crystal glasses and silver trays overflowing with tiny bite-sized sandwiches and delicate cream cakes. They moved in and sat down gingerly on velvet chairs and sofas. But the room finally was not full. Not many people had come to mourn her son. Only his wife and the few friends who had remained with him to the end, through the last, the bad years. This had taken strength, tenacity, and a large measure of loyalty, loyalty of the durable irrational kind – an anachronism amongst reasonable people with more important priorities.

They sat silently these last few friends, awkwardly at first, self-consciously pulling off gloves or smoothing their dark clothing, but she, his mother put them at ease.

"Do you remember..." she said, recalling her son as she too pulled the gloves from her white, still smooth hands.

"Do you remember..." she said, retelling the stories they all knew, drawing them back with her into the good times, the brief uncertain good times. Occasionally as she spoke she bent down to pat the dog who had thrown himself at her feet. He still rolled ecstatically every time she touched him, wagging, it seemed, his whole body.

Then capably she poured sherry and handed it from a silver tray. Thankfully they drank; it was an excellent sherry. Each individual breast was warmed and heartened by its fire. They all became a little less stiff, less formal under its sway. Nevertheless, it came constantly to mind that burying a son, an only son and so young, was not an easy thing to do so gracefully, it took courage. It took courage also to prepare the room as she had done. The polished tables reflected the flowers sent for convention's sake, or to comfort. They were fresh and beautiful, not a single petal had fallen and their scent filled the room. Under one glass vase filled with white roses stood a picture of her son set in a silver frame. He was smiling carelessly as he used to, secure and handsome and so young. The mourners looked away. It is hard, they remembered, to bury a son. Hard and unjust to give birth and to bury a son. But his mother was strong and brave. They saw it in the way she held herself, upright and straight, in the way her hair set in careful waves fell neatly around her face; her face, composed, normal, almost as though nothing out of the ordinary had happened. She had borne the service stoically, no tears had glinted in her eyes, her shoulders had remained stiff and square.

Now she smiled indulgently at her dog as he jumped onto a sofa. He looked charming, head cocked, eyes bright as he watched her, waiting it seemed for a rebuke.

"He is so naughty," she sighed as she stroked his head forbearingly and smiled when he licked her hand, "I suppose I spoil him." She poured more sherry and did not seem to notice as the dog secretly snatched a cake from a tray and swallowed it hastily. He continued to sit quietly amongst the mourners, watching them carefully with his small dark eyes and licking the cream from his lips with a wet, pink tongue.

Beside another vase crammed with carnations and jasmine stood another picture, a more recent one, of her son and his wife – a casual snapshot taken at a picnic in a garden. They sat a little apart, under a lush leafy tree which shadowed their faces as they looked out into the sun. He held a glass in one hand and smiled, past his wife, past the photographer into the distance. There he was – as young as before but with his face already showing traces of puffiness, the over-indulgence which, towards the end, badly marred his looks. His mother followed the mourners' eyes. He looks happy there I think...but more than that she could not say. The picture had been taken on one of the many days on which she had not been present, on one of the many days the mourners preferred to forget. His wife turned away, towards the likeness in the silver frame, the likeness she tried most often to recall, to remember best. The dog on the velvet sofa scratched, sniffed and slyly licked cream from the empty tray.

The mourners' glasses were empty too, the afternoon was ending, the ritual would conclude. Slowly they gathered their things and began to murmur their farewells, guiltily, for now they were finally obliged to leave her alone. Alone with her flowers and her pictures. Guiltily, for they were alive. She led the way to the door and out into the garden. As she opened the gate the dog darted between their legs and in a moment was on the footpath.

"Come here at once," she called to him and scolded loudly, "you naughty boy – here, I say – at once." But the dog ignored her. He behaved as though he was entirely alone, as though she did not exist. They watched as he sniffed his way along the gutter, lifting his leg here and there and pushing his snub nose into piles of dead leaves. Slowly and deliberately he wandered further and further away from her. She called again but not even an ear twitched. She started after him then, hurrying on her sensible heels. When he heard her footsteps the dog stopped and turned to look at her. She stopped too and tentatively held out her hand. They looked deep into each other's eyes, the dog with his head on one side as though summing her up. Then with a bound he leapt away from her and out into the road, legs racing and ears flying. The car, as it came around the corner, caught and tipped him, bowling him over and over like a hoop, and then sped on. It was possible that the driver did not even see him. The dog lay on his side in the gutter, quite still, only the breeze ruffling his fur. One of the mourners ran to pick him up but the small shape was not, after all, completely limp. Slowly he opened his eyes and lifted his head. The dog was a little dazed, but clearly, after a thorough examination, entirely unhurt. Thankfully, ceremoniously he was returned to grateful arms.

"You naughty dog," she said fondly. "You are very very lucky, why, you might have been killed." Subdued, the dog gently licked her face.

"Thank heavens he's alright," she said to the mourners, and then, "I suppose I should control him more but it's so difficult – he enjoys everything so – I simply haven't the heart to stop him."

"Goodbye," said the mourners, "goodbye..." and she waved to them, trying to control the dog who was becoming more lively now after his fright and struggling, struggling for release, trying to evade, as he soon would, the grip of her lenient arms.

THE SMELL OF JASMINE

IT WAS a modern divorce – an amicable divorce. As amicable as it could be when one party is consistently, blindingly and hurtfully honest, as amicable as it ever could be when a husband leaves his wife for his secretary. Thus, Peter left Gina and their good friends, the Clarks, looked on.

The Clarks were a remarkable couple, solid and united like bread and butter and equally as inseparable. No one ever called them Alan and Fay, they were simply the Clarks. They had married long ago, few could now remember the day and by all accounts had lived, and were living, happily ever after. Theirs was an old-fashioned marriage and as such thrived on old-fashioned virtues. Thrift for one. Their house was in a good but not the best area. Not over-large but comfortably roomy and well-furnished without ostentation. One or two original paintings hung on their walls, painted by some of the more minor artists. Fay dressed smartly and was resourceful enough to make most of her own and her children's clothes, an accomplishment of which Alan was inordinately proud; as they were both proud of their two well-planned, gifted children who were attractive, industrious and did not take drugs. Fay had been doing a part-time course for some years now, in social work. "Human Conflict is my bag," she often said, and added, "helping people is what it's all about – it makes me feel good."

Sometimes Fay even found time to play her flute. It is easy to see why many people envied them. Morality, another old-fashioned virtue, also clung heavily to the Clarks. No breath of scandal of any kind had ever touched them. There had been no sordid – or, perhaps worse, serious – love affairs, no deceptions, no betrayals, nothing at all for their friends to discuss in hushed tones over drinks as friends are inclined to do given the least opportunity. Or if there was something once, the Clarks weren't saying. No wonder they were envied. They were the kind of people for whom nothing ever seemed to go wrong, to go bad, not like in other more ordinary people's lives. The worst they ever admitted to was a cold, an occasional bout of flu, or even rarer a hangover, all of which they faced with courage, on the surface at least, and overcame with ease.

The Clarks entertained splendidly and often. Fay cooked superbly; she was renowned for her curries, good and hot, made from the cheaper cuts of beef or sometimes chicken, and also for her mouth-wateringly complicated desserts – her creme caramel was justly famous. As for Alan, he could always be relied upon to produce at least two bottles of his better wine. Not that he was in any way mean, merely careful. "Good wine should be savoured, not tossed down like lemonade," he often said. The combination of guests too was invariably successful because the Clarks always gave the matter of their choice a good deal of thought. Judiciously they mixed engineers with artists, doctors with actors or journalists, conservatives with socialists (both of the armchair and the militant variety), and even Protestants with Catholics. Whatever the occupations, political affiliations or religions of their friends it mattered not to the Clarks – men with beards or without were all welcome at their table. Often, too, those chosen were quite important in their own Fields. Thus, over the French Provincial dinner set (picked up for a song in the Dordogne) there was always just enough intellectual banter to stimulate without giving offence. No one had ever, or it was clear would ever, come to blows across one of Fay's soufflés. Liberal thinkers but calm and serene, that was the essence of the Clarks. And serious – they took things seriously, in particular the divorce of their dearest friends, Gina and Peter. It grieved them to see what they thought of as a successful marriage break down in such a trite fashion. But Fay was there immediately and it was only natural that Gina should turn to her for support.

Gina and Fay shared a long association, they were known as close friends. Indeed, Fay was a good friend to others as well as to Gina. She was known to be wise and kind and an authority on the management of most of the basics of life, like babies, husbands, herbs and cakes. And she shared her knowledge generously. Fay was regularly first with news of confinements, terminal diseases, or a death, and first with flowers, out of her own garden of course, so much more thoughtful, so much nicer. Needless to say, Fay could be relied upon never to forget a birthday. She was, in fact, generally reliable. And happy. No one had ever seen Fay depressed. The word did not exist in her vocabulary, as she often announced when she heard others complain. She was always ready to cheer up the less fortunate of her friends with jolly stories of her children's latest successes, such as dancing as a butterfly in the school concert (Fay had made the costume herself) or prizes for Latin and Mathematics. Fay's stories were never boring because she only related achievements and in her family, there were many. She was never heard to grumble about her husband, her garden or her cleaning lady, an achievement in itself. Fay thought deeply about people and their relationships but never lapsed into spontaneous emotional outbursts which might wound – she was eminently tactful. Similarly, in Gina's distress, when in her initial wretchedness she had packed a bag and fled to Fay, Fay took charge with strength and consideration. She became Gina's comforter and confidante throughout the immediate and most difficult time. Gina talked and Fay listened. Fay fed her. and pampered her. She made every effort to see that Gina was not left alone to grieve though, ever practical, she realized that some grieving had to be done. "Time will heal..." she encouraged, and slowly and gradually helped Gina to accept the reality of her loss of Peter, that it was final.

They often sat in Fay's kitchen and over coffee and Danish pastries (hot out of Fay's oven) examined the situation from all possible angles. Then Fay was very careful to be scrupulously fair, to Gina and also to Peter. Because being such a good friend to both she had quite naturally been available for Peter, had helped him too over the most distressing period. During a number of small luncheons she had listened to Peter's woes and had advised on his best course of action, one which would avoid hurting Gina too much, though some hurt inevitably could not be avoided she had to agree. Of course she had advised him on how to deal with Mandy, his new love who was under the misconception that as soon as Peter left Gina, life for the two of them would be all roses, and who was surprisingly bad-tempered when she found it was not quite as she had planned. Tactfully, Fay kept these matters (and the luncheons) from Gina. She did not want Gina, in her present highly emotional state, to misinterpret her concern for Peter, to see it as some kind of betrayal – which of course it was not. It was simply far too early to burden her with Peter and Mandy's problems as well as her own.

The topic of Mandy had been, in the main, studiously avoided by Fay, if not by Gina who was eager for any news at all, but who was made to understand that Fay was not being evasive, merely considerate. Whatever Fay did was for Gina's own good.

Later, when Gina was finally established in her lonely flat and hating it, she would occasionally and diffidently ask Fay about Peter. Fay was still careful with her answers, she particularly did not want to hurt Gina further by reviving harmful (as she saw it) memories. But the day eventually came when she was forced to confess – or rather when she considered that the time had come to be completely honest. When Gina could at last "take it".

It was a spring day, windless and quiet and they were walking in Fay's garden and admiring the jasmine. "Peter and Mandy?" Gina asked. Afterwards, whenever once a year in spring Gina smelt jasmine she was sharply reminded of Fay and their walk in her garden. Fay's jasmine was carefully trained to climb the verandah post which it had dutifully done until it reached the roof. There, instead of letting it burgeon and flourish wildly and untidily as jasmine usually does, Fay had pruned it heavily and tied single strands to grow in single file, trimly like soldiers in formation, horizontally along the beam. It was pretty but sparse. They walked on towards the rockery and the many small colourful plants Fay nurtured so carefully. A fiddly garden thought Gina privately, not enough trees. One was always obliged to look down at the ground in Fay's garden.

"Peter and Mandy..." Fay repeated, and placed the sprinkler in the middle of the lawn. "Well yes, we did have a small dinner party for them last week. Alan was keen to see Peter, he misses him such a lot – you remember how well they got on." Fay turned the tap and the sprinkler began to revolve and make rainbows in the sun. She continued, "And Peter has been rather miserable, you know how he gets." She lowered her voice sympathetically, she knew Peter so well. "Guilt feelings of course – quite natural in the circumstances but totally unnecessary at this stage." Gina said nothing. "Come this way, look..."

They picked their way along a path bordered by impeccably flowering azaleas in various shades of pink and white. Fay went on confidentially, "It's not a very happy situation for poor Mandy."

"Why?" asked Gina surprised out of her silence.

"Well, Peter gets so moody at times, you remember, which is quite understandable of course," she added hastily, "but poor Mandy sometimes finds it a teensy bit difficult to cope." "And poor Mandy..." Gina steeled herself finally to ask, wondering how close Fay and Mandy had lately become, "Mandy – what do you think of her, really?"

"Why don't we go and sit on the verandah, under the jasmine and be comfortable," said Fay.

"And poor Mandy?" repeated Gina when they were settled. Fay could no longer avoid the question.

"Oh well, Mandy..." She patted the pretty patchwork cushion she had made herself and prepared to be the tactful as well as omniscient authority. And fair – that was the main thing. "She's very pretty of course... a little younger than you, though that's not important at all naturally..." "Naturally," echoed Gina, "... and?"

"Well..." Fay thought deeply. "She is modest and unassuming and for all that reasonably clever – not as intelligent as you of course."

"Of course," said Gina hearing the bees buzzing in the jasmine.

"You see..."Fay sighed hugely. "I have avoided talking about Mandy because I simply didn't want to hurt you, but now that you're pressing me – I hoped you wouldn't actually – I'll have to. Believe me I tried not to like Mandy, for your sake, but eventually I had to be honest with myself for all our sakes. I began to feel guilty, guilty that I was beginning to like Mandy too much. But then I examined my motives. (Fay often examined motives, hers and others – it was a result of her training.) I suspected my motives, examined them and found them unsound, even unreasonable. After all, guilt feelings are the most destructive feelings one can have. I must admit it. I was weak – I usually handle my emotions better than that. So I pulled myself together. I didn't want to fall into that trap, the trap of guilt – it's so utterly destructive."

Gina was forced to admire Fay's adroit handling of her own emotions. How wonderful to have such few and such easily resolved doubts – how convenient. Fay continued. "You must understand that my friendship with her is not nearly as profound as my friendship with you Gina – I had to be honest with myself and with you. And Alan feels the same way of course."

"Of course," echoed Gina again, there seemed to be nothing else to say.

The shadowy figure of Alan had not imposed itself on Gina at all. He would hug her solicitously whenever she came to see Fay and then disappear into his study looking faintly embarrassed. (Alan never looked more than faintly anything.) He left the job of comforting to Fay. "She is so good at that sort of thing, much better than me," he always said. Whenever he joined Gina and Fay for a meal he avoided any mention of Peter and Mandy. He behaved as though nothing untoward had happened at all and told Gina some of his funnier stories to make her laugh. (He was much in demand as an after dinner speaker and had an endless fund of amusing stories to tell.)

"And now what about a cup of tea?" asked Fay, preparing to close the rather untidy conversation. She rose. "Frankly Gina, I must tell you I feel sorry for poor Mandy."

"You do?" asked Gina, remembering that Fay often felt frankly sorry for people, she had a tremendous capacity for compassion of that kind.

"Yes I do, even though I must admit she complements Peter so well, she's exactly the sort of person he should have married – but you're better off without him really," she added hastily, seeing Gina's face. "And anyway, there are plenty more fish in the sea, remember that." She left Gina with the bees and the jasmine.

"There are plenty more fish in the sea," Fay repeated when she returned with the Earl Grey, "and I propose to find some for you."

Assiduously she began to invite Gina to dinner to meet one or another of her pet bachelors, with all of whom she was on kissing and hugging terms and who all praised Fay and her cooking, her clothes and her charms, mercilessly. They loved to go to the Clarks, often accepting

41

an invitation at only a moment's notice and drinking Alan's better wines with relish. Gina gradually came to understand, from the petting, the cuddling, the sexy chaff and ribbing that invariably took place for most of the evening that Fay would always be on more intimate terms with these accommodating gentlemen than Gina. Even though Fay was working so hard to bring them together, to bring some romance back into Gina's cruelly deprived life. After all it was only natural – Fay understood it so well and repeated it as often as she felt it was necessary – that when a man leaves a woman for a younger and let's face it, prettier one, she feels rejected, terribly insecure. She doubts her femininity, she must fight hard to regain her self-esteem. After one of these evenings, one which had proved to be rather more fun than most, Fay pointed out (as a friend, solicitous for her welfare, nothing more) that Gina, in her present unfortunate position, must not throw herself at these bachelors. The last thing Fay wanted to see was Gina's reputation harmed in any way – Gina really could not afford to attract that kind of gossip at this moment. Gina found it easy to agree with Fay and to dine more often with bachelors who were not on such intimate terms with the Clarks. She occasionally refused an invitation to the Clarks.

After a while Gina no longer asked after Peter and Mandy. She knew the Clarks were seeing them but they saw quite as much of Gina. In these matters they were still punctiliously fair and nowadays Fay, honest as ever, made a point of mentioning it. After all, Gina had well and truly "got over" the whole dismal affair. It was so simple to tell her "we had dinner with Peter and Mandy last week" or "Mandy came over for lunch yesterday, she's looking much better now" and so forth. The more she mentioned it, the more Gina began to wonder what on earth Fay and Mandy had to say to each other. Was Fay perhaps comforting "poor Mandy" with anecdotes of hers and Peter's incompatibilities and murmuring how sorry she felt for "poor Gina"? Was she giving Mandy a rundown on her psychological state or an analysis of her motives? Or did they merely walk in the garden and discuss pruning. Maybe they talked about the weather. One thing was certain, Fay would never say anything derogatory or mean about her – she was definitely to be trusted on that score. Fay, in her own words, was not disloyal. She was well-known for her refusal at all times to enter into back-biting hate sessions about any of her friends. "Alan loathes cattiness in women," she often declared, "he simply won't allow it." It was quite impossible for Gina to imagine her saying anything as illogical or unsound such as "Peter is a shit" or "Mandy is a bitch". Harsh words, even about politicians, never crossed Fay's lips. All this notwithstanding, Gina began to feel an inexplicable mistrust about confiding in Fay as she had ungrudgingly done for so long. There was also the incident of the trifle, Peter's favourite pudding which Gina used to make. "Mandy would like to know how you make that trifle," said Fay casually one day. "Will you write it out for me and I'll give it to her? She wants to make it for Peter – it's his favourite." As though Gina had forgotten.

For the first time in Fay's presence Gina became vehement. "Certainly not – I wouldn't dream of letting her have it."

Fay looked at her silently for a moment, then gently, as though encouraging an invalid said, "I didn't realize you were still harbouring such bitterness – you mustn't succumb to that, it's so bad for you." And repeated, "I do hate to see you so bitter."

Gina wrote out her recipe for trifle and gave it to Fay. Afterwards she felt curiously lighter, as though something had been finally shuffled off. Like the snake its skin. She emerged and guiltlessly began to see less of the Clarks and more of her less worthy friends – those who had blindly taken sides (hers) without reservation. Those who agreed with the intellectually unacceptable (to Fay) precept, "My country right or wrong." Those who agreed that Peter was basically a shit, and who had other explanations for Mandy's behaviour which were not quite as understanding as Fay's. Those who even suggested that Mandy was not the paragon of all the virtues she appeared to Fay and who laughed heartily when Mandy contracted a particularly recalcitrant and itchy case of eczema; though it was no joking matter for Fay who felt very sorry for Mandy and treated her diligently with herbal tea.

On the increasingly rare occasions when Gina visited the Clarks, Fay with her proprietorial ways would quiz her about her latest men friends. Then Gina found it easier to be vague. She felt disinclined to tell the Clarks, Peter and Mandy's good friends, anything exceptionally intimate. She found she had less and less to say to the Clarks, sometimes there seemed to be nothing left to say at all. These feelings caused her twinges of guilt until she realized that Fay did not take it amiss. Fay hardly noticed. Certainly she was unmoved and recriminations which Gina had unconsciously expected did not follow. Peter and Mandy too, it was rumoured were seeing less of the Clarks whose wonderful dinner parties continued unabated, by all accounts, with other perhaps equally as important friends.

Sometimes, at Christmas cocktail parties, the catching up with the yearly gossip time, couples who had known Peter and Gina when they were together and who had lost touch after the divorce, would ask the Clarks for news of them. The Clarks, their best friends, were bound to know. Then Fay, never forgetting to imply how intimately she knew both Gina and Peter, would retell (briefly) and in the reverent tones she used for important events, the sad tale of the divorce. She always finished up saying smugly and with justifiable pride, "Alan and I have a perfectly clear conscience – it wasn't easy but we stayed friends with them both."

MOONSHINE

THEIR EYES met across the room. By the time he had pushed his way past the chattering cocktail party people to reach her, they were both laughing.

"Some Enchanted Evening," he quoted ironically.

"More disenchanting I think," she said, "I can't imagine why I came."

"Well I'm glad you did," he said, and got her another drink.

They talked and gossiped, discovered mutual friends and demolished some of them cruelly. They began to like each other and after still another drink, came, more volubly, to more intimate discussion. It was astonishing how their thoughts on all manner of subjects were reciprocated – or intertwined delicately and so beautifully. Around them the chattering people became noisier, even more intrusive, superfluous. Eagerly he asked her to have dinner with him.

The martinis were pale and cold. Delicious – they agreed. She gave him her olive. He liked olives, she did not. This, so far, was the only point on which they differed. But what a tiny difference and in any case it didn't matter. It couldn't matter, not when they understood each other so well – their minds reflecting each other's like the clearest of mirrors.

For instance, why was Mozart's music so perfect? She said because it was the mean, the middle path. It had a little of everything, without wallowing in any one emotion. He added that it was passionate without excess, that the deceptive simplicity of the notes could not disguise its extreme sensitivity, its wholeness, its subtlety and tact. Looking into each other's eyes they decided that it summed up a view of life at its most complete.

The avocados were ripe, pale green and creamy. The sauce vinaigrette was not quite right. Too much vinegar perhaps but delicious in spite of that. They discussed life in terms of Mozart, in terms of people. They liked people – oh yes – but not very often.

"The world is full of nice people," he said ironically.

"With hearts of gold," she added.

They laughed; how they hated the cliché, how they despised the obvious.

With the cannelloni and their wine-flushed cheeks they came to Wagner. Passionately, her eyes shooting sparks from the candlelight, she hated Wagner. What a vulgar composer, how he luxuriated in layers of sticky soggy emotion, like a cream cake," she said, "too rich, almost nauseating." He felt just the same.

"And doesn't people's taste in music reflect their deepest attitudes to life?" he asked, and continued "The emotional response to music must be instinctive and cannot really be hidden. A basic response." They agreed – so easily.

And now coffee, the right ending to an excellent meal. They sighed contentedly – in perfect accord.

She thought she had never seen anyone quite so handsome. She thought that he was possibly the most perfect man in the world. She smiled as she hugged the cliché, secretly.

"What are you thinking?" he asked.

"Oh nothing," she said and lowered her eyes.

In the candlelight he saw that she was entirely and remarkably beautiful. He would have liked to tell her so but could find only the most obvious of words. Sadly he remained silent.

He paid the bill and they left the candlelight and the delicious smoky smells and stepped into the cool warmth of a summer night. Their footsteps echoed on the pavement, a contrapuntal echo she thought, my two steps to his one, but in tune, in time. He wanted to take her hand but she was swinging her coat with it, bemused – disinterested it seemed to him.

The car stood in a dark space between two lampposts and when they reached it they saw a thousand moons, some big, some small, reflected in the chrome, on the windows, the door handles, everywhere. They looked up and found it, hanging heavy and full between two tall buildings.

"Oh look," she said, "the moon is full."

"Yes," he said briskly, too briskly it seemed to her, so that her sigh was stifled arid she curved her mouth ironically.

"But a bit too obvious?"

He could only agree. The dazzling reflections in the doors and windows shimmered, wavered and broke up as they got into the car. There was nothing left to say. Silently he drove her home, while the moon rose high and silver into the sky – quite beyond their reach.

ASSASSINATION '63

AFTER HER husband left her for the red ringleted little hairdresser from Hendon, Mara and her son aged four and three quarters came to San Francisco to live for a time with Ruthie, Morrie, Debbie aged four-and-a-half, Danny just two and the baby. The apartment was on the first floor of a tall clapboard halfway down the hill from the Medical Centre where Morrie worked. He walked to work and left the car (wheels appropriately curbed) for Ruthie to use during the day.

The apartment was long and thin and appointed like the carriage of a railway train. The big living room in front with its bay window overlooking the steepness of the street was where the children sat on the floor in front of the television eating rice bubbles and watching Captain Kangaroo. Then there was the long hall with rooms opening out from it like individual compartments of a train all the way to the room at the end where the children slept in double bunk beds. Mara's bed was the sofa in the front room where at night the light from the street lamps kept her awake and thinking.

Mara and Ruthie drank a lot of coffee in between doing the unavoidable, essential things that had to be done to keep four children alive. They complained about the chores, they bemoaned their lost freedom. They talked of their boredom with housework they talked and talked while they fed the children frankfurters and potato salad and pizza and hamburgers. The baby, up on the table in his bouncer sucked on his bottle or on his pacifier. The blue and white plastic pacifier often fell out of the baby's mouth onto the floor but Ruthie just picked it up, wiped it on her sleeve and thrust it back into the waiting mouth. Together Mara and Ruthie dieted, trying to reduce the bulges consequent upon childbirth. They followed a book called "Key to Lasting Slimness" and counted calories (when they had time) and hardly cheated. They ate tuna salad and chicken salad and sometimes when they had been very strict with the diet for a day or two, cheese cake and chocolates. They smoked. Ruthie only when Morrie wasn't there. Morrie did not approve of smoking. After dinner while sipping the duty-free Courvoisier Mara had brought from London Morrie nagged her to stop smoking. He brought her pills that would make smoking taste bad. "Now is not the time to give up smoking," said Mara but she pretended to take the little red pills and then told Morrie they didn't work. She went on smoking. The children too smoked passively, but who knew that then?

On fine sunny days, when there was no mist drifting in from the ocean, Mara and Ruthie took the children to the Golden Gate park and sat by the merry-go-round – the one featured in the film "Days of Wine and Roses" the one with the beautifully carved and colourfully painted wooden horses. The children played nearby and Mara and Ruthie sat and smoked and talked. They told each other everything they could think of about their past lives – their love affairs in college, their dreams. They told each other everything, no secrets except that Ruthie did not reveal that Morrie, when he lost his temper which happened quite often, sometimes hit her. Confiding in Ruthie and trusting her, Mara thought Ruthie was telling the absolute complete truth all the time and so she was, merely leaving out that one truth. It was only many years later that Mara discovered that truth – that Morrie had been violent, only occasionally but still; she should really have guessed because she had seen Morrie's violent temper in action. Once when bathing the children, all in the bath together and fighting as children do, he had hit her son, (probably like he sometimes hit Ruthie,) on the head. The child's screams echoed down the long hall and Mara wept and packed her bags but Ruthie persuaded her to stay. Morrie apologised.

One day they drove to Palo Alto where a new adventure playground for children had recently been built. There were huge complicated wooden frames, bright red and blue plastic shapes for crawling under or climbing over and through, swings and benches and tables for picnics. Being November, it was beginning to be cold and Mara wore her brown suede coat. At the end, when she left San Francisco for ever, she gave it to Ruthie. Suede is very long lasting, perhaps she wears it still. Mara told Ruthie many truths about the red ringleted girl who had stolen her husband. Blatantly stolen him away making no bones about it – the girl had said so. She had told Mara's husband that she had as much right to happiness as Mara which could hardly be doubted. The child's future did not feature at all in the red ringletted head. Ruthie was as sympathetic as she could possibly be. They discussed the many painful tortures they would perform on this girl if only they could and laughed at their fancies. Mara laughed but through bitten back tears.

It was a mere two years later that Ruthie performed a kind of torture but not on the red ringletted girl. Mara was the recipient of the pain when Ruthie and Morrie became friends with Mara's ex-husband and his new wife – the red ringletted girl, hair no longer red, (too vulgar said Mara's husband) it was now, according to reports, golden. Ruthie and Morrie accepted the invitation of a trip on their yacht to the island of Majorca which was an irresistible invitation everyone agreed. It was not until Ruthie stopped writing to Mara (now far away in another country) that Mara heard from a friend about the events in Majorca. Mara did not believe the rumours and wrote asking Ruthie for an explanation. Ruthie was fair and above all unprejudiced – a quality of which she had always been exceptionally proud. She wrote Mara a long letter. She told Mara that the golden ringletted girl, now wife, was very pretty, (younger than Mara of course) and really perfectly charming. She wrote that Mara had been quite wrong about this girl in San Francisco though it had to be admitted, (Ruthie was always fair) she was not quite as intelligent as Mara.

In San Francisco Mara and Ruthie paid a baby sitter so that they could go shopping alone without the children. They went to Union Square, Ruthie took her to the fabulous ladies room with the golden fittings at I. Magnin and they had lunch at Trader Vic's. The diet was forgotten for the day as they drank Mai Tai's and ate exotic salads and chicken with peanut sauce. They talked about the irresponsibility, the foolishness, the distressing behaviour of Mara's husband. They talked about the future and Mara's chances of regaining her husband. Their two minds thought alike on every subject particularly on love, marriage and the boredom of repetitive housework. They had a unique relationship they knew. They had a fine, infinitely satisfying time together.

When Morrie went away to Palm Springs for a three day conference the first thing Mara and Ruthie did was to go shopping to the supermarket. The children dragged behind as usual, the baby dropped his pacifier but Ruthie just rubbed it with her hand as always and put it straight back into the complaining mouth. The children took candy and chocolate from the lower shelves where they were stacked for just this temptation except the ruse misfired because Ruthie being very strong-minded refused to pay for the open boxes even though the children had begun to eat the candy. She merely dumped them on the counter and told the check-out girl in no uncertain terms exactly, where she should have put the candy – that is out of reach of children. Mara admired her ruthlessness.

They took the shopping bags and the whining children back home and then, while the baby was still crawling laboriously up the stairs (he always arrived eventually) Ruthie put the frying pan on the stove. Into the frying pan went the bacon they had purchased and soon the irresistible smell of frying bacon filled the apartment. Mara and Ruthie fell on the crisp lengths with relish. The children received merely the usual frankfurters. Morrie forbade any kind of pork in his house. His parents had been without prejudice or fanaticism in the matter of diet. They had eaten ham and pork with impunity, as a matter of course and

Morrie, to be different, to spite their beliefs perhaps, became a curmudgeon in the matter. He revived the rituals of the religion, against Ruthie's wishes or beliefs. Mara did not understand why Ruthie acceded to these observances. Ruthie explained it was easier to agree – perhaps she was avoiding an unpleasant, even violent confrontation. It certainly caused her no pangs of conscience to break Morrie's laws when she was able. With the bacon taste still lingering on their lips they discussed the ruthlessness of the red ringletted girl who had stolen the father of Mara's son. Her shameless use of sex to entice him away, her basic stupidity. She was after all only an uneducated hairdresser.

From Majorca where the climate must have been temperate, the ever forgiving Ruthie and in all fairness, wrote again to Mara repeating that the golden ringletted girl was actually very intelligent, not as intelligent as Mara of course, but quite acceptable in discerning company. Mara, unbelievably hurt by these inconceivable events, wrote, challenging Ruthie to explain her disloyalty. Ruthie wrote sincerely again that she felt no guilt in the matter. Guilt, wrote Ruthie, was such a destructive emotion; she had no intention of falling into that trap. Safe on the deck of the yacht with her new friends, Ruthie wrote, "you must not be so demanding of our friendship, after all, loyalty of the order of "my country right or wrong" is not a concept I can accept" She wrote "you must not be bitter, you must not let Her come between us." She justified herself entirely to her own satisfaction. Remorse, or even the smallest sign that Mara was still in her heart, remained stubbornly absent. In Majorca, Ruthie drank Mara's ex-husband's champagne with a clear conscience.

In San Francisco after lunch they peeled fruit for the children and when Ruthies daughter turned blue from choking on a large section of orange Mara saved her life by turning her upside down and hooking the piece out with her finger. They took the children to the park again and they talked and smoked and enjoyed simply being together. Mara read "The Cat in the Hat" and "Green Eggs and Ham" to the children before their bedtime and they all laughed immoderately and begged for more.

Once again, for the last time as it turned out, Ruthie and Mara hired the babysitter and left the children (with sighs of relief) to go shopping. First they stopped for a late breakfast of waffles and crisp bacon and maple syrup. They sat up at the counter in a coffee shop and heard with disbelief the shooting and death of President Kennedy. Stunned and saddened by this shocking event they did no shopping at all.

At home the next day in between washing the dishes they saw Jack Ruby on. television gunning down the suspect Lee Harvey Oswald. Momentous almost unbelievable events; events never to be forgotten.

Two days later Morrie and Ruthie took Mara to the airport for her flight home to Sydney. Both Ruthie and Mara's eyes were wet as they embraced, swearing (unnecessarily) eternal friendship and promising to write always and often.

Mara and her son waved to Ruthie and Morrie and the children as they crossed the San Francisco tarmac. No one, least of all Ruthie and Mara, imagined then, that everything had been for the very last time.

THE GAME

DODGING ROUND the trees every now and then seemed to hold him off a bit, though he was incredibly accurate with the pistol.

The irritation she felt at being so ignominiously caught by each jet of water as he squirted it increased in proportion with her breathlessness. The jets shot through the hot air like small silver needles, pricking unpleasantly icy on her bare arms and neck, and she shivered with fury as the urge to protect at least her face, grew into a kind of panic. Faster, faster she ran, sandals flapping, scratching her palms on the mulberry tree each time she swung round it; and now there was a stitch in her side jabbing painfully with each breath.

Useless to run; there he was coming from her left, the black pistol pointing with malevolent accuracy at her flushed face. Quite useless. She cringed, watching from under a protective arm as his finger tightened on the trigger, waiting for the humiliating stream of water. But surprisingly nothing happened. The pistol was empty. Tom shrugged and turned to go back to the house. There was derision in his slow casual slouch; even his back seemed to mock her.

Julie lay down flat on the grass in the shade of the big tree and reflected bitterly on the unfairness of Nature in bestowing Her gifts of strength and speed with such partiality on the male sex.

It was not even cooler here, and beyond her piece of shade the gums shimmered grey in the heat haze.

Lately the process of growing up had been very much to her disadvantage. In the past she had been able to run as fast – no, faster than Tom, and climb trees and rocks with the same facility; in all their games they had been well matched. And now disconcertingly, she had become inferior. Soon her mother would be able to say with quiet satisfaction to her friends, "Julie used to be such a little tomboy you know, but now I'm glad to say..."

And there seemed to be no compensations at all. Even this beloved frock, faded pink by the sun, dusty now from the grass on which she was sprawled, and undeniably too short, would soon have to be discarded. She watched the verandah where Tom would shortly reappear and in her impotence drummed her heels hard on the prickly grass. In the tree above her the mulberries showed red like beads between the leaves and hung and danced on their branches as the westerly warmed them.

The screen door banged and Tom appeared, pacing deliberately slowly towards her. She decided this time to face him. Running away was simply an open invitation to be chased into another humiliating damp surrender.

Round the rusty sprinkler jerking monotonously beside the dry flower beds he came, across the lawn softly like an Indian on the warpath. With some red and green feathers in his dark hair, she thought, the illusion would be complete – an Indian evilly stalking his helpless prey. She rose to her feet crouching slightly and tense. When he realized that she was not going to run Tom hesitated, with the pistol held high and ready, and in that moment Julie jumped forward and snatched it from his hand. Before he could recover she was streaking away towards the mulberry tree. He was after her immediately, a small smile starting on his face. He liked her courage and this turning of the tables was, after all, only momentary. He even slowed down a little as he approached the gun levelled at him from behind the tree.

Julie squeezed the trigger – and missed. Tom easily dodged the silver stream, laughing cheerfully, patronizingly it seemed to her. She shot at him again and again, pulling the trigger more and more fiercely, and in her fury missing, and missing again. Nothing could shift the grin on his complacent face, and when the gun was empty again he waited confidently for her to give in. Instead she ran towards the house, hiding with her back the effort, scarlet on her face, of smothered tears. She reached the verandah and kicked the door open. The crash as it banged shut echoed angrily across the garden.

Tom followed more slowly; he could afford to save his breath. He would corner her in the kitchen where she would be reloading the pistol.

In the kitchen Julie turned the cold water full on and let the sink fill up. She put the pistol into the water and watched the tiny bubbles rising slowly from the nozzle as it filled. She breathed more quietly now and the water was cool on her wrists. When she heard his step on the verandah she turned to face the door, holding the dripping pistol so tightly to her that it made damp patches on the pinkness of her frock.

He stood by the open door, hands carelessly on his hips, the anticipation of triumph already in his eyes.

"OK Julie," he said, "give it to me."

"No," she said, and her voice did not tremble. "Get back or I'll shoot." He watched her, summing her up. Would she dare? Then, with a quick movement he stepped into the room and before she could think, was grasping her arms tightly. She could not move at all; she, who not so long ago had been able to knock him down and keep him pinned helplessly to the ground. The game was really over – and lost.

"Do let me go," she begged quietly.

"If you promise not to shoot," he replied tolerantly.

"I promise."

"Word of honour?" His blues eyes looked straight into hers.

"Word of honour."

He let her go and stepping back laughed aloud. His laughter echoed round the tiled kitchen and flew into her face like a gust of hot wind. She lifted the pistol with both hands and fired it straight into the brown laughing face.

Tom gasped in shocked disbelief; in his eyes wide and blank with surprise, Julie saw herself reflected, pale and shamefully small. The water running down his cheeks looked like giant tears.

PREJUDICE

"I'VE NEVER liked the Germans," said Steve.

"Oh come now," I said, "how can you generalize like that? It's not sound – a man of your intelligence."

"But you must admit that my background inclines me to a highly proper dislike of them; an almost mandatory dislike in fact." He paused. "After all..."

"After all," I replied heatedly, "you didn't suffer, you were only a child in 1940 and lucky enough to be able to grow up here in Australia in peace. I can understand you having an emotional hangover because of your family's experiences but surely now after all these years you must have acquired a more sanguine attitude?"

Steve was listening patiently. "I know," he said, "and you're quite right; we've both heard these arguments before and while I subscribed to them rationally for a time – "He paused. "Let me tell you just how hard I did try to rid myself of what in essence is simply a prejudice – or rather was. Now I no longer know what to call it. As a matter of fact I'm even afraid to examine it too closely."

I settled myself more comfortably in my chair, prepared to be tolerant of what I felt sure would be a highly emotional story.

"As you know," Steve began, "after I finished at the University I went to London. From there I often toured the Continent – as we all did – but I avoided Germany, I found the German tourists I had seen in other countries quite intolerable. Loud and brash, mostly fat and always rude. Oh yes," he smiled, "prejudice again – and so I told myself that I was not being fair, that I was being a stodgy fool. I had to go and see for myself. On my way to Switzerland, one year, I travelled through Germany. I found that at home in their own country they were different, quite unlike the tourists I had seen elsewhere, and gradually I lost a feeling I had had about them, a feeling I didn't realize was a part of my dislike until I lost it. To put it quite simply – it was fear. It became clear to me now that as a Jew, as a child of Jewish parents who had been driven out of Hitler's Europe, I had disliked Germans instinctively and fearfully, and realizing this my fear became, instead, indifference.

"That year we went to Kitzbiihel, four of us, all students. We'd been put up at a small *pension* just outside the village and every morning we tramped along the road, the sun striking sparks off the snow, to the practice slopes. There we pursued two sports: skiing and – just as exciting and exhilarating for us – hunt for girls. And there were so many.

"English girls with big fur hats and big teeth. Pert French girls chattering deliciously in scrappy, sexy English. There were loud tough Australian girls on cheap tours from London and plump German girls with large behinds who sped down the difficult slopes faster than anyone else. We hunted them all; on the snow during the day and in the smoky *kellers* at night. We hunted them furiously and sometimes successfully.

"I met Helga in my second week. Someone brought her to the table where we were eating sausages and drinking beer in the sun. She was fun – perhaps a trifle earnest, but she laughed even when she didn't see the joke – and she was attractive. To be quite honest I had not been as successful as my friends in the hunt for girls and at this time I was becoming the butt of their frequent and obvious jokes. This was beginning to rankle and when the not unattractive, though German, Helga began to single me out, I responded with an at first contrived, but soon real, enthusiasm. It was only once that I nearly wavered. The conversation after dinner touched on the war – touched only lightly, but when Helga murmured something about "our glorious armies", Bob jumped on her immediately.

"What on earth do you mean?" he snorted rudely, "you lost didn't you?"

"Helga shrugged lightly. "But of course – it was inevitable – everyone was against us."

"Her eyes were wide and innocent and silenced even Bob. I poured more wine and changed the subject. I told myself hastily that during the war she'd been very young. I thought of tomorrow, when my campaign – that of persuading Helga into my bed – would be successful. Our last afternoon too – I was anxious not to lose my advantage. So we danced, I remember, probably till dawn.

"After lunch the next day we tramped companionably on the hard-packed snow back to my *pension*. We giggled a little as we crept secretly up the back stairs to my room. After we'd removed our heavy boots we lay on the huge feathery eiderdown and talked for a while. Helga told me she had a fiancé in Germany. She thought she would probably never marry him because "the bed" – she patted the eiderdown smartly – "was not very good". The fiancé it seemed worked hard and was "always too tired". And then Helga quickly and efficiently removed her clothes and folded them neatly onto a chair. Surprisingly, I was not put off by this story or by her actions – on the contrary – I was grateful to her for making it all so easy. She slipped into bed and watched as I in my turn took off my clothes. When I stood naked, about to step into bed, Helga's eyes suddenly widened with shock.

"But you're a Jew," she said, sitting up in the bed and pulling the eiderdown to cover her bare breasts.

"Yes," I said, waiting, and as I watched her face it became slowly expressionless. After a few seconds, seconds in which still no further emotion of any kind appeared on her face or in her eyes, she shrugged in that strange, matter of fact, almost lifeless fashion of hers and efficiently turned the bedclothes invitingly back.

"Helga asked me to visit her on my way back to London," Steve concluded, "but I didn't go. I never went back to Germany again."

BLOOD

HE WAS told to call them Grace and Arthur. His parents had demanded it. Grace and Arthur were not consulted on the matter and did not really seem to mind very much. Sometimes Grace raised her eyebrows in a way she had when he called her by her name loudly, in the park or on the street, raised them as though to say it has nothing to do with me what my grandson calls me. Then she would take his hand, condescending carefully to his smallness – Grace was good with children – and say mildly, "William you should not shout quite so loudly in public," and they would walk on together quite companionably.

At the kindergarten William told his teacher that he had no grandmother or grandfather. She was a kind girl, and felt sorry for him and avoided talking to the class about grandparents whenever she remembered, until the day Grace came to the school to pick him up. It was a Tuesday, the day Grace always had her hair done and she looked very elegant (she subscribed to *Vogue* of course), every inch a real grandmother. William's teacher, a discerning girl, took stock and said stiffly, "Well, it seems we've been telling some little white lies, haven't we William?" Grace raised her eyebrows and said "Of course it has nothing whatever to do with me, it's his parents, they have these funny modern ideas and there's nothing I can do about it is there?" and laughed lightly. His teacher laughed too.

Later, when he told his parents what had happened they laughed too, but really laughed as though they were quite sure it was all really funny and not like Grace and his teacher had laughed. It was a puzzle but they explained it to him. How Grace and Arthur, as well as being Daddy's parents and thus his grandparents, were also people, real people and had names. Not just any Granny or Grandpa, real people like he, William, was a person and had a name. Would he like to be called just Child? William agreed that he would not like to be called Child. He always remembered that day; it was the day he had acquired grandparents of his own, just the same as all the other children at the kindergarten, and it felt reassuring.

Grace and Arthur had a unit, overlooking the harbour, which they kept obsessively tidy. It was full of old furniture and fascinating bric-a-brac which Grace and Arthur had collected over the years; with inlaid boxes, porcelain figures and glass birds on highly polished tables and careful bowls of flowers everywhere. The flowers were mostly imitation, but very expensive Grace said. They looked incredibly real, huge bunches of white gardenias nestling in shiny green plastic leaves or tall red silk roses in sheafs. "So convenient," said Grace, "they never fade, they never die, and I don't have to change nasty smelly water." Grace was wonderfully fastidious. "Aren't they simply marvellous?" She also said, "It's the effect that counts, that really matters." On the window sill a pair of blue Victorian vases with long crystal drops threw a cold light onto the floor. Beside them, on Arthur's antique desk with the tooled green leather top, there were framed photographs of Arthur shaking hands with important people, while Grace, smiling gently, stood by his side.

William liked to visit Grace and Arthur. They let him do anything at all, even jump on the sofa with his sandals on which he was not allowed to do at home. When his mother said, "William stop that immediately," Arthur would say, "Oh leave him alone dear," and look at her disapprovingly. He was good at looking disapproving and this made William feel uneasy. So he would become more boisterous and naughty and Grace and Arthur would laugh and tell his mother that she was too strict. They allowed William too much ice cream and too many sweets and fizzy drinks which his mother said would rot his teeth and Grace and Arthur said, "You fuss too much dear, leave him alone dear."

When William was tired of jumping on the sofa or on the big leather chair he would stand by the window and watch the boats on the harbour. Sometimes he was allowed to look through Arthur's binoculars, even though they were very heavy and his mother fussed about him dropping them, while the others sipped their drinks and talked, or Arthur talked.

"Blood," he often said, when he wasn't deriding an associate (Arthur had a sharp, malicious tongue), "is thicker than water. Look at William, look at the way he holds those binoculars – the image of my Uncle Jim."

"But he's got your eyes Arthur," Grace might say, "and Mary's nose of course."

"And the curl in his hair and the colour – just like Vera's." They discussed William in this way as though he was an object only recently and advantageously purchased. William by the window felt like a visitor in their lives, a listener and not part of them at all even though it seemed to be important, this discussion of his shape. They discussed it in such intricate detail, their heads speculatively on one side or another as they searched for confirmation of resemblances. His character too was not his own but partly Arthur's, Grace's or that of some other obscure relation William had never seen. A relation always belonging to Grace or Arthur; his mother and her people were never mentioned at all. The blood, it appeared had emanated entirely from Grace and Arthur – perhaps the water than which it was thicker came from his mother's side of the family.

Grace and Arthur hardly ever visited William's house, they were much too busy. William thought they were very important people, always so busy with other important people about whom Arthur could be very funny afterwards. He crucified his friends gaily and with remarkable facility, was intolerant of their mistakes, mishaps and even their smallest errors. Arthur capitalized on disasters. William's parents laughed a great deal when they visited Grace and Arthur.

They were always so busy, struggling along, Grace would say, their lives revolving around the large, square, gilt-edged invitations which were regularly displayed on their mantelpiece.

Sometimes William brought pictures he had made and coloured in for Grace and Arthur but they hardly seemed to notice. "That's nice dear," Grace would say, "and now have some more cake." They took much more notice when William was being noisy and boisterous. On his birthday they always gave him money. "So much easier dear," said Grace, handing over too many crisp notes, "and he can buy exactly what he wants." William and his mother banked some of the money in William's own bank account and they spent some of it together, but afterwards he never remembered what they had bought. The only thing he remembered Grace and Arthur ever giving him was the carnation. Once when his mother took William to see Grace and Arthur, Grace was making flowers out of multi-coloured tissue paper. Carnations, she explained to William, and let him help. They drew large circles on the paper and cut them out with Grace's big silver scissors. Then Grace took some of the circles and bunched them carefully in the middle, making a stem out of picture wire and then pulling and tucking the petals into shape. When a flower was finished William was allowed to put it gently, so as not to squash it, into the large vase Grace had prepared. The carnations, all made of different colours, were beautiful, so bright and luscious and very nearly real, except for the blue ones.

"Effective, don't you think?" said Grace who was making them for some of her friends for Christmas. "And so fashionable this year dear," to William's mother. William was allowed to choose one to take home because he had been such a help to Grace. He chose a big red one and buried his nose in it. "It smells like paper," he said, "but nice." "It's the appearance, the effect that matters," said Grace.

His mother pinned the carnation to the corner of a poster on the wall of his room where it looked very pretty. William could see it as he lay in bed and it reminded him of Grace and Arthur.

But after William's parents were divorced Grace and Arthur faded gradually from William's life; somehow they seemed to be busier than ever and he saw even less of them than he had done before. On the rare occasions his mother, doing her duty, took him to see them, Grace and Arthur were exceptionally quiet. They whispered and spoke in hushed tones about things William was not supposed to know; like the divorce, and whose fault it was, and how it was all to be expected since "she was never really one of us", which he heard Grace mutter to Arthur one day as his mother stood by the window looking at the boats on the harbour and biting her lip. "But it doesn't make any difference to us dear," said Arthur "you must come and see us often," and once a year on his birthday they sent William a cheque which came in very handy as he was growing up and saving for record-players and bikes.

One day his mother said to William, now nearly grown up, "You don't want this any more do you?" and took the faded carnation off the wall. It had only faded a little, Grace always used the very best tissue paper. The carnation reminded William of Grace and Arthur. "Why," he asked his mother, "don't we ever see Grace and Arthur any more?"

"I think," said his mother, "though I'm not sure, that Grace and Arthur have cut you out of the will of memory; you remind them of things they would, in their world, rather forget. It's the effect you see, you have the effect, not your fault of course, of reminding them of a mistake; perhaps even of a failure." She paused and then went on briskly "Although really I think they're just too busy, you remember how busy they always were. They'd love to see you I'm sure," and she threw the carnation into the bin.

William did not understand his mother, he was not listening very carefully, mainly because he did not really care. There was, after all, very little to remember about Grace and Arthur. He remembered jumping on sofas, looking at boats through Arthur's binoculars and too much ice cream. He remembered the endless discussions of his character and shape and he remembered Arthur saying, too often, something about blood.

But the faces of Grace and Arthur eluded him.

FINE BONES

MY DEAREST friend Kitty, with her dark head bobbing and hazel eyes blazing, nods emphatically. "Of course they exist, how can you doubt it – Unidentified Flying Objects, that is UFOs, do exist; it's been proved, scientifically, well practically anyway . .

"Nonsense," says my husband Sam, putting more wood on the fire.

"But it's true, there's a book..." Kitty is so delightfully illogical when she becomes excited.

"Go on then expert, enlighten us," says Sam solemnly.

"Oh shut up Sam, stop teasing." Kitty is laughing.

I watch them arguing in the firelight. She is so beautiful, the glow from the fire lighting up her high cheek bones. Fine boned, elegant Kitty, more delicate, more beautiful than I could ever hope to be.

"All right," Kitty is shouting at Sam now, "I agree with you. Those people who tell about trips in flying saucers with little purple men *are* nuts and I don't believe them any more than you do, but that doesn't mean that UFOs don't exist – they do, they do – it will all be revealed when they think we're ready."

"Kitty," my husband is laughing indulgently, "you are a dear sweet Kitty but entirely and completely mad. Another cognac?"

Kitty is furious. She jumps up and throws her hands about. "Wait and see," she prophesies, "just wait and see, clever Sam."

He jumps up too and takes her wrists, her fine-boned wrists in his strong hands. "Calm down then – my little seer – calm down."

I see her breath catching and then she is quiet. She sinks back into the cushions and her lashes fall onto her flushed cheeks. Then they smile, softly, secretly together as the rain runs down the pane in long wet lines. We sip our cognac and the fire burns red.

"Such things don't exist," I tell them, "I don't believe in any of it – not for a moment – it can't be true." And I sigh, while they laugh together.

"You should believe," says Kitty, my friend, my dearest friend Kitty... "It would make a difference." She is defiant now.

"What possible difference could it make?" I ask – but I think I already know. Sam prods the fire.

"It's a good day for a fire," he says.

Kitty warms her hands at Sam's fire. "A perfect day for it – just right. Sam, how can we convince her?"

And she looks up at him, pleading, looking like an angel in the firelight. Sam looks down at me sadly. I will him with all my strength not to tell me now, not today, not yet – please not yet.

"Another day Kitty," he says, "you will persuade her that UFOs exist but let's skip it for today."

Kitty's eyes drop, she shifts in her chair and wriggles her feet.

Sam continues, "But you know she does believe in telepathy and telekinesis – the power of mind over matter – all that supernatural stuff."

"It's not supernatural at all," I tell him, "it's a phenomenon that's been investigated just as scientifically as your UFOs, Kitty."

"Has it really?" Kitty is sceptical. "Like that man from Israel who can bend spoons – what do you think of him?"

"Uri Geller?"

"Yes – do you think those things he does are possible?"

"Oh yes – I think they're highly possible."

Sam laughs scornfully. "Rubbish! I think that man is either a very clever magician or a charlatan and I incline to the latter view."

Kitty smiles. "Of course he's a fraud – no one can move solid matter with his mind – it must be a trick."

"No it's not," I say, "I think you can do anything if you want to enough."

I see the rain running wetly down the pane. It is cold outside, very cold. "I think it's all possible and I think Geller is quite genuine. Have you seen him on television? He's quite remarkable to watch."

Kitty yawns. "Yes I've seen him – and I turned him off. I thought it was so boring just watching spoons and keys and things bending and turning and breaking. I'd much rather see a UFO – now that would really be exciting, and more useful too, for mankind and all that. What possible use is bending spoons?"

Her eyes are shining as she looks at Sam for confirmation.

"You little idiot," he says and it's as though I'm not there at all. He is enchanted.

"It's late," I whisper to break their spell. "It's late."

"Oh yes – I suppose I must go." says Kitty reluctantly.

Sam helps her up out of the chair. When their hands touch I can feel the burning on my skin too – it hurts – how it hurts.

"Don't come out – you'll get wet," Sam tells me.

They go out into the rain, to Kitty's car. The wind is howling and blowing and bending the leaves on the trees. "Tomorrow," I feel them whispering to each other. "Tomorrow." So it will have to be tonight. I can't bear it any longer. It must be tonight. Sam comes back to the fire. Back to me.

"What are you thinking, my dear? You look so solemn." He is saying it as though he is afraid, as though he may regret something.

"Just sleepy, so sleepy," I say, "let's sit and watch the fire burn down – let's not even talk." He is relieved.

He sits down comfortably. He is putting off what he thought he would have to tell me. I see him putting it out of sight, tidily, on a shelf at the back of his mind. The excitement of Kitty has subsided, now she is gone. We sip cognac and gaze into the fire.

I can see Kitty driving home through the rain. She is happy. I can feel her happiness, her certainty, it fills the car – she is singing. I sit and warm my cold hands at the fire as Sam dozes, and I can feel it, her certainty, curling round my heart like a vine, greenly, icily, twisting and choking me. Underneath it all my strength is growing – I will need it now. I will use it now. The certainty of my own strength fills me and warms me. Kitty is at the top of the long hill. I see her, singing, the road winding down, wet, in front of her, and now, finally, I am the stronger though she will never know it. I am sad for her – sad that she will never know it, my poor friend Kitty. Sam rouses me.

"You look pale and tired."

Oh yes,– exhausted – my strength has left me. In bed, I fall immediately into a deep dreamless sleep.

In the morning, a bright shining morning, we read of Kitty's death in the paper.

"The cause of last night's fatal accident in which a woman died is being investigated. It was found, after examination of the wreckage, that the ignition key of her automatic sedan was in the "off" position. How this occurred is unknown. A police spokesman stated that many people appear to be unaware of the fact that turning off the ignition while travelling in a car with automatic transmission may lock the steering wheel and also render the brakes inoperative."

Sam is shocked.

"What a terrible thing... how ghastly... it must have happened just after she left us... she was so... so alive."

But his arm is around me, he is comforting me. I can feel his sadness but I can feel, too, his relief. There would have been demands, perhaps too many, despite the intoxication, and I am comfortable and good for him. His arm tightens around me.

"Poor Kitty, I wonder if she turned the key off? Maybe she did it to save gas; she said she was a bit low when she left last night."

"Yes – perhaps that was it."

"And I suppose most women wouldn't know the dangers of turning off the ignition in automatic cars?"

"I know," I tell him. Outside the sun shines in a clear and cloudless sky.

Even without my dearest friend Kitty I am never bored – I can always see her fine fleshless bones, see how white they look, and pure, how slender, how fine – see how they clatter and click as I turn them... and turn them... and turn them...

BIRTHDAY

SHE STRETCHED and felt the apprehension creeping into her body. The day had been reached, it had arrived; no major disaster had happened to prevent it and however far away and unreal it had once seemed, that impossibility had been overcome. Thirty years old, half a life – perhaps more than half – she tried to hold the thought, to make it mean something but it receded, then faded. "Get up," she said aloud, feeling the impatience, the striving, the unease. On every day, tomorrow throwing a brighter shadow – tomorrow I will capture the answer, the meaning, the perfection which is sometimes there.

From the attic window she watched the sun going down slowly; slowly the twilight came seeping into the room, blue and grey and clear above the lights beginning to sparkle across the water. She could see the bed and his profile on the white pillow, beautifully asleep, dark and pale in the twilight.

She sat up, impatiently trying to throw off the memory of that particular perfection. Today it did not move her – perhaps it never would again. When she looked out of her window she saw the sun shining through a light haze. It was going to be another grey, hot day, to be concluded, she thought listlessly, by Elizabeth's birthday dinner. Just the four of us – as always – like a family, gossiping, boring and tolerating; celebrating events, disastrous or otherwise, together, bound by the stronger-than-blood ties of time.

The grey hot day became a dark humid night. Condensation on the crystal glasses made the wine look unclear and misty but it tasted deliciously cold.

"I think I know Teddy better than any of you," said Colin. Madeleine sitting on his right at the round table on the verandah felt that it was a plea. The expression of sardonic amusement which usually accompanied Colin's remarks about Teddy was missing from a face which had suddenly, unbelievably almost for Colin, softened. But perhaps it was only the candlelight.

"After all," he continued, "we were always together in those days, our favourite years if you like – first parties, the first girls."

Madeleine remembered Teddy's endlessly repetitious stories, wildly funny at first, and hoped that Colin would not dredge them up once again. There had been too many years in between. The tentative advances, the embarrassments, had become with the nostalgic recalling and retelling of them, bold deeds – triumphs of youth. But parodies now, she thought. Already we are old.

Mrs Williams over the groceries this morning: "Thirty years *young* my dear." But we are old, old and have hardly begun.

She smiled at Colin. "Perhaps you do know him best," she said, thinking that after all he ought to – two of a kind. She sighed.

Oliver finished spooning soup into his wide smiling mouth and proclaimed seriously, "Yes of course you do." He didn't mean it; he wanted a comfortable dinner.

Colin leant back in his chair. He was gratified. Elizabeth expertly removing the plates, added that Teddy was really very sweet. Madeleine shivered, sweet – he had always been so maliciously pleased to hear bad news of Colin.

"Poor old Colin," he would say, "why doesn't he pull himself together; wasting his life in that irresponsible fashion." And he would shake his head ruefully, patronizingly and relax, and being Teddy he would then add, "Of course I can't help feeling pleased, "Schadenfreude"," and he would laugh, even more pleased with himself and his use of the German word correctly pronounced.

Elizabeth put the silver dishes on the table. *"Coq au vin"* she said proudly.

"It smells absolutely delicious," said Oliver.

Madeleine looked at his face shadowed in the candlelight and wondered if she loved him. A square face, the lips a little too full, the smooth dark hair receding slightly from the broad forehead; conventional good looks, a smug and pampered face. But when he smiled that ridiculously ecstatic smile, it was as though a window were being opened into a view of a unique -and mysterious landscape. She wanted very much to explore that landscape but he withheld it; he hugged it to himself tenaciously, almost meanly.

They began to eat. A small breeze had sprung up but though the candles flickered and danced, it was as hot as it had been all day. The lights along the wide curve of the bay, just visible behind the houses opposite, flickered too and beyond them stretched the darkness of the harbour. Looking out into the darkness across the candles, Madeleine felt again that familiar, weightless sensation of time telescoping and reducing into the single, pinpoint well that was her life, complete to this moment. As though all the emotions of the past returned, distilled in one clear drop, intensely sharp, and yet she herself detached, watching from the wrong end of the telescope.

Emotions, feelings rather, of complete happiness so rare and of pain, loss, anticipation and disappointment. And all those feelings repeating themselves and repeating and becoming over the years, if not less intense, easier somehow to bear; experience behind them? And all these feelings bound up with men and love and nothing else. Nothing else that really mattered anyway. She had fought against this bald, obvious truth so often and had found no way out. It had to be finally admitted that life was nothing but the man one loved, the men one had loved (nostalgia – another such intense pain-pleasure feeling), and the men one was going to love in the future. And these last were almost always best until they became present and reality. She ate the food on the plate in front of her, hardly tasting it. The dark endlessness of the harbour stretching away to nothing over the candles strengthened her feelings of time stopped, time waiting it seemed, waiting for her to remember past time, so much of it wasted, so little used.

The room was full of mirrors, behind the book-lined shelves, on the walls and on all the doors from floor to ceiling, everywhere.

The desks, each with its telephone and litter of papers, looked incongruous in this room which had once been the Duchess of Something- or-other's bedroom and was now merely an office. Left alone, Madeleine sat down by one of the desks and waited. It was still in this room and peaceful and the late afternoon sun fell in dusty squares on the parquet floor. She watched her reflection looking back at her from the wall, from the door, then from the far door, smaller. She rose to look at the books and her reflection moved with her; Madeleine wherever she turned, wherever she looked, the red coat swinging, her hair shining and smooth, her face serious – waiting, content to wait, for whom?

Remembered pieces of time, were they really the valuable pieces? Whole years with Teddy vanished; no part of them came back spontaneously as having been lived fully and with awareness, together. All the years like layers and each layer in more layers like a rainbow cake of events and emotions. And of the million forgotten people and things, why just these remembered vividly, suddenly, like being stabbed? Stabbed into life by a million more insignificant things, words or sounds or glimpses of half turned faces.

Some to stab just once; others to stab again and again in the layers of the years, with exactly the same intensity.

Colin settled back into his chair and began to light his pipe.

"Now," he said, "Teddy would have enjoyed this so much – " The breeze stirred the candles and the women's hair. Warily Madeleine looked at him. He is preparing to give us a wine- sodden but maliciously perspicacious summing up, she thought, of Teddy, whose mind never touched mine; like the same poles of two magnets able to come so close that it seems they must touch but finally and inevitably pushing each other away.

She smiled at Oliver who was assiduously, as though performing a service for her, turning the conversation away from Teddy. Or was he uneasy for himself in case Colin's corrosive tongue should light on him?

"Let's have some music," he said enthusiastically, "after that splendid meal and on such an auspicious occasion." He laughed at Madeleine. "What shall we have?" Not waiting for a reply he went into the sitting room.

Sandy spirals of irritation crept through her; confident happy Oliver, tied and wrapped securely in his charm, in his invulnerability, locked in his own avowed uninvolvement. Inhuman Oliver, she thought fiercely, gently but firmly detaching one by one the clutching fingers of those who tried to touch, to move him. It was the gentleness that was deceptive; so often had she mistaken it for tenderness.

Four people at the round table by a window overlooking the lights. Who were the other two and were they really there eating the cool pale green avocados with silver spoons and with music from the other room that was almost palpable in its glorious flow – Octavian presenting the silver rose to Sophie, ecstatically? Someone said inconsequentially, "They always play it at weddings, what is it?"

"Oh Perfect Love, "said Madeleine ironically.

"Oh Perfect Love, "repeated Oliver softly, and in the sky the rocket exploded into purple and gold fragments and fell silently as they watched. When the music came to its sublime end they sighed, almost with relief.

"Perfect, "said Oliver, and brooked no argument, "but perhaps a little too sentimental, no?"

"But we must keep some of the illusions, "she said, her eyes begging him to give her back the perfection. He smiled distantly.

They could hear him now, in the sitting room, sliding the record out of its cover, putting it on the turntable and then the soft hiss of the needle. He appeared at the door, head bent a little, waiting. Suddenly, tumultuously from behind him, sounded the effervescent whooping horns of *Rosenkavalier*. He smiled.

"I thought this more apt – tonight," he said. Madeleine felt as though she had been turned swiftly and severely upside down. She felt violated, by the music which swept across them out to sea and by his eyes which had become, while he looked at her, transparent, tender.

They drank their coffee and listened, all of them becalmed. The music anchored reality. Cheap tawdry reality, glittering like a glass necklace on the neck of a woman, dulled now, cast off.

Perfection thought Madeleine fleetingly and then even that thought disappeared, the telescope shrank to nothing and was gone and she existed only in the darkness and the music.

Later, when in an island of hard clear starlight Oliver bent his head softly to her mouth, she thought, now it is beginning, really beginning; but she shivered as she saw the starlight glitter coldly through the moving leaves and disappear.

SWALLOWING GOD

ISABELLA WAS different – something she began to understand the longer she was at the convent. She was different because her father was not a Catholic, which of course at the convent was the best and only thing everyone ought to be. She was different, although not as different as the two truly non-Catholic children who were greatly pitied by the other girls – they lived nearby which was probably the only reason their parents sent them to the convent. She was not as different as the two girls who had no mother, both even more to be pitied, since they were thought of as rather odd; as though the possession of only half of a family was their own fault, the situation being unenviable and quite unimaginable for all the normal girls. She was certainly not as different as the poor girl whose parents, it was whispered, could not afford to pay the convent fees and who was there only because the charity of the nuns allowed it. It was said she brought a penny once a week to give to Sister as her token fee. This thought was repellent to Isabella who wondered how the child could subject herself to such a humiliation, and how Sister could accept such an offering, or even worse, perhaps demand it. So Isabella had company in her difference, but no comfort. And there were so many other things – like her name which was not Mary or Bernadette or some other simple or saint's name. Isabella understood that her name had a bold racy flavour merely from the way Sister sometimes said it, particularly when she chided her for naughtiness. Certainly no one else had that name – only Isabella alone. She even knew where babies came from which was more than most of the other girls knew, and Sister knew she knew, having once come upon a small group in the playground, arguing vehemently. Isabella was just saying scornfully that babies were definitely not found under cabbages or rose bushes – surely everyone knew that they came out of mothers' tummies, when Sister appeared.

"Isabella," she said smoothly, giving her a long look, "we don't discuss things like that here."

Isabella was different, she stood out. She wished very badly that her father would instantly and miraculously become a Catholic, it would have made many things much easier for her.

Isabella was a weekly boarder. Every Sunday, although she asked them to, her Catholic mother and non-Catholic father did not take her to Mass. She dreaded Monday mornings when Sister Gertrude would bail her up against the plumbago hedge after chapel and ask the inevitable question.

"Isabella, did you go to Mass on Sunday?"

Isabella would shuffle a little but it was no use lying to Sister, besides she knew anyway and sometimes Isabella wondered why she bothered to ask at all.

"No Sister."

Sister Gertrude always sighed heavily, as though it was her own sin with which Isabella was burdening her. Then she would deliver a lecture, always kindly, on the evils of sin, of mortal sin, and especially of the evils of that particular mortal sin. She expounded at length on the dangers to which Isabella's soul was being exposed, and on its imminent descent, straight to hell, should a car knock her over or some other fatal accident suddenly occur. None of this frightened Isabella or even made much of an impression. She was not yet fully aware of the implications and consequences of sin, nor did she connect herself in any way intimately with a soul. She was much more aware of the inconvenience of being made late for morning tea, by the undue length of Sister's lecture and of missing her slice of bread and jam.

She did however understand that she was different and not at all a good girl and was therefore pleasantly surprised and excited when she found herself included, since she was already seven years old, in the prestigious First Communion class; the event to take place in three months' time.

Before the longed for consummation of the Communion, however, would come Confession – formal and official introduction to Sin. Now, Sister Gertrude told them, switching into high gear, they would all realize the gravity and responsibility associated with Sin and most portentous of all, its grave and dire consequences. Thus the second lesson every morning (the first being Catechism which had to be learnt by heart and was really quite easy even if most of the questions and answers were exceedingly mysterious and mostly incomprehensible) was devoted to Sin and the Soul.

Sister Gertrude rarely explained, she indoctrinated. The children did not ask questions, they were not expected to. They accepted everything Sister told them as though the words fell from the lips of God himself. She instructed the class in the difference between venial sins and mortal sins and the effect on the entry of the soul into, firstly, earthly states of grace and, subsequently, when the mortal body was dead, into heaven or hell. Hell was fire and brimstone only by repute, though the possibility was always there and had to be taken into serious account. Hell's main torment was the eternal deprivation of the presence of God.

Heaven was infinitely more desirable because there one would be, for all eternity, in the sight of God. Eternity, said Sister, was a length of time which was not measurable; for instance, if the earth were made entirely of lead and a butterfly brushed it once every million years with its wings, then when the earth was completely worn away, that day would be the first day of eternity – an awe-inspiring thought for the class.

They learnt, too, that the day of their first communion was to be the happiest day of their lives, because they were to receive God into their bodies and souls. In order to receive him adequately the soul was required to be in a state of grace, which meant entirely free from sin, and so they came to confession, confession which conveniently washed away any and every sin.

Sister introduced them to the basics of the ritual in its practical application, with special emphasis on the soul once again, and now, every week after chapel, they were allowed to stay behind with the older girls and wait for Father to hear their confession. To confess their sins – sins which were sometimes hard to find even though Sister had explained it so often. What were sins? Sins were pride and vanity and selfishness and greed, difficult concepts for a child of seven. Easier to understand were talking in class, whispering in chapel, making too much noise or laughing too loudly. But these were only grey venial sins, not black mortal ones like Isabella (who was sometimes held up to the class as an example) committed every Sunday, even though inadvertently committed it seemed, but only to Isabella, not to Sister or to God. She began to worry about the state of her soul, which, had Sister known her private thoughts, would probably have pleased her.

Isabella thought of her soul as a sort of large tablecloth, situated inside herself somewhere in the area between her neck and her navel. After confession it was a pure gleaming white. As the week progressed and Isabella sinned, the tablecloth became increasingly and progressively greyer in colour, with here and there an odd black spot for a particularly bad sin. A missed Mass on Sunday caused the whole cloth to turn quite black, completely imposing itself on the lesser sins – taking over as it were. But then came the ease and relief of confession.

First the kneeling in line in the dimness of the chapel, sniffing the faint and solemn scent of incense which always lingered in the air, left over from Mass, all quiet except for the sounds of girls rising to enter the darkness of the confessional to kneel in front of the grille behind which sat Father (invisible) murmuring in Latin when the ritual "Bless my Father for I have sinned" was intoned. Then the list of sins, carefully gleaned from the week's activities, with Father often helping when explanation became difficult. And then the absolution, Isabella feeling positively lighter, feeling the tablecloth inside her becoming whiter and whiter as she emerged to kneel again in the front pews to say the penance Father had imposed. Usually three Our Fathers, and three Hail Marys and then out again, into the sunshine as light and bright as her soul. The devil thwarted and outwitted again. Sister Gertrude spent a lot of time talking about the devil, how pleased he was when one sinned, how he always lay in wait for miscreants, tempting them to the further excesses upon which he thrived. The devil – formerly the brightest of the angels, now fallen. One of the holy pictures in the classroom showed God casting him out of heaven. He looked very beautiful in his shimmering blue armour.

Gradually Isabella became more serious than ever. She worried not only about the state of her own soul, but also that of her mother's, who, unlike her poor non-Catholic and thus damned father, was nominally a Catholic but, for incomprehensible reasons, not at all inclined to go to Mass on Sundays. Isabella took her aside one day and gravely explained that she was committing a mortal sin and, in case of sudden death, would go straight to hell – not for her any lingering in purgatory (that strange and dismal place full of pale, unbaptized babies, or was that limbo?) where at least prayer (Isabella's) and suffering (hers) would eventually ensure a place in heaven. Her mother laughed, though she was very impressed with Isabella's knowledge, laughed (how that would have horrified Sister) and assured Isabella that she had a private arrangement with God and Isabella should not worry in the least about her soul's damnation, her soul was fine.

Isabella was not convinced that Sister Gertrude would accept this notion of a private arrangement with God and sensibly kept her mother's assurances to herself. After all she had done her best, like the missionary Sisters of old, she had attempted to convert the natives. Now she worried only about her own soul, since Sister was concentrating much more on Isabella than on the other girls who did not seem to be nearly as naughty. Only Isabella – most different, the naughtiest of all.

Had she not been the only one to positively refuse to eat her lovely piece of boiled pumpkin at lunchtime last week? Sister had made her sit in the refectory in front of it for two hours after the other girls had gone; had let her sit, watching it congeal slowly on her plate, pale, cold and slightly green around the edges. Unwillingly Sister finally had to give up and let her go. The starving children in Europe would have gobbled it up she said sorrowfully – Isabella was shamefully wasting good food, as well as being entirely and utterly disobedient. Disobedience – there was another sin to tell Father.

Sin – it was clear to Isabella that it was not possible not to sin. Merely being alive seemed enough. Even the Sisters sinned, Sister Gertrude announced piously one day (unthinkable as this was to the girls), but of course very rarely although they all went to confession even more often than the girls. It was a matter of much speculation amongst the class, though an answer was never settled upon, exactly what it was the Sisters did wrong that they then had to confess to Father. Whatever it was would have to be quite accidental or inadvertent, certainly not on purpose. (The devil would hardly have a chance tempting Sister Gertrude – that was sure.) After all, Sisters were like God, swooping about the playground like swallows, their skirts hitched up around their knees out of the dust showing their black ankles as they supervised the children's play, throwing balls and dealing out sins like lollies. Those sins they could more easily understand.

"Don't snatch", "don't shout", "don't hit (horrors) another girl", "don't push in", "wait your turn", "don't poke your tongue out at your friends Isabella, the very tongue on which you will soon receive the host – Body of Our Lord!" The sin of rudeness – oh dear, how easy it was indeed to sin.

During the last week, the last before the longed for day of the First Communion, preparations went ahead frenziedly. White dresses had their final fittings, veils were trimmed and hemmed, and black shoes and floors were polished to shine like mirrors. All the Sisters seemed to be on edge; they were over-excited as though preparing for a wedding. The day was so important, the happiest day of their lives they repeated, returning in memory to their own day and relating it in detail to the girls – oh so lucky girls they stressed, almost enviously.

Then came the memorable hour on Wednesday when Father came to the convent, especially to hear the confessions of the First Communion class. He came for the twelve small girls alone, so that their souls would be whiter than first snow and more full of grace than a chocolate eclair full of cream. Lessons were suspended and they filed solemnly into chapel for the occasion. How important they felt with the whole school looking on, the younger girls envious, the older ones smiling indulgently as they too remembered their own special day.

By Friday, excitement was electric in the air. The whole class felt it – they became boisterous and talkative, and Sister, not unusually in these circumstances, was less patient than normal.

"Settle down girls," she said sharply to the noisy class. The children ignored her.

"Settle down at once," she said, more loudly this time, again with no result. Perhaps they simply did not hear her. She looked around the class for an instigator, a focus of the disobedience and soon found it.

"Isabella – stop that chattering immediately."

Isabella, engrossed in a conversation, did not hear her. She was explaining the complexities of a card game played with holy pictures to Philomena and Philomena simply did not understand. Philomena, thought Isabella, exasperated, was definitely dim.

"Isabella!" Sister almost shouted this time. "Be quiet at once!"

Isabella still did not hear her above the general hubbub – she and Philomena were laughing now. Sister's face went purple.

"Silence girls!" she shouted, at the same time clapping her hands vigorously – and suddenly there was silence.

"Isabella," Sister hissed, "you naughty girl – you bad girl! How can you be so disobedient, so rude and so selfish on the very eve of your First Communion? You have stained – stained – "she repeated, almost wailing, "your soul with your unforgiveable behaviour!" She threw her hands up in despair. "Whatever am I going to do with you now?"

Half an hour later Isabella, dressed in her Sunday tunic, panama hat and blazer, found herself being marched down the convent steps and up the road to the bus stop. Sister Gertrude had taken charge, had merely said, "Something must be done – you certainly cannot make your First Communion in your present graceless state." Then she maintained a stony silence all the way on the bus and also on the short walk to a house set in the beautifully kept gardens beside the church. There she knocked on the front door and when a maid opened it said firmly that they had come to see Father.

Isabella was puzzled, she did not understand what was happening. However throughout it all she felt more bewilderment than fear and certainly no remorse. She had come to accept that sinning, when she did not mean to, was part of life, her life anyway, since she was different. Since no matter how hard she tried it seemed she was quite incapable of being good like the other girls.

They waited silently in the hall until Father appeared. "Well" Sister," he smiled, "what can I do for you – and isn't this one of my First Communicants?"

"It is Isabella," said Sister Gertrude ominously, as though the mere mention of that name would explain all.

"Yes?" asked Father.

"Isabella," said Sister in a doom-laden voice, "has sinned. I am sure you would not want her to make her First Communion in such a state so I have brought her to you now, for confession."

Father wrinkled his brow; he looked from Sister to Isabella and back again. Then he took Isabella by the hand. "If you'll wait here please Sister," he said and led Isabella away down a long hall. To the church and the darkness of the confessional thought Isabella. Instead Father took her to his study. It was a large, light, rich room, with shiny parquet floors on which lay deep red and blue Persian carpets. Books lined the walls – it smelled deliciously, sinfully, of tobacco. It was, thought Isabella surprised, very like home. Father sat down on a comfortable sofa and put Isabella beside him. "Are you comfortable Isabella?" asked Father.

"Yes Father," said Isabella – she felt very much at home.

"Now tell me," continued Father, "what you have done that has upset Sister so?"

Isabella, leaving nothing out, told him. "Well," said Father after a little consideration, "it seems to me that you didn't really mean to be naughty, is that so Isabella?"

"Yes Father."

"I don't think God would see it as a sin – I think He has already forgiven you and I am quite certain that He would not want you to go to confession again. You did come to me on Wednesday didn't you?"

"Yes Father."

"Then that is all that is necessary."

Father and Isabella chatted for a little while about ordinary things, about her school work, about her friends, about swimming which she loved and when he took her back to Sister they were both laughing.

"Here we are Sister," said Father, "here is Isabella – she is a good girl, a very good girl." Isabella glowed. "I don't think she will give you any more trouble."

On the way home a slightly mollified Sister invited Isabella, tactfully, to give an account of herself but Isabella refused to be drawn. She felt benevolent towards her and even somehow superior. For once she knew something Sister didn't. Fundamentally however, she did not really know what to make of any of it, and consigned the whole strange experience, like sin itself, to those areas she knew were beyond her immediate understanding. One day, she thought, it would all become as clear and logical as the sums she could do so easily in class.

Sunday was a sunny, golden day. The twelve small girls, hair curled into corkscrews under their snowy veils, filed apprehensively and excitedly into chapel to kneel in the very front pews, as the organ played and the choir joyfully sang. Behind them sat friends and relations and both Isabella's parents. Father, in festive white and silver vestments began to say Mass and the twelve small souls bowed their heads devoutly.

Soon it was time to file to the altar rail, to kneel and to wait for Father to give them the Host from his golden chalice. When her turn came Isabella dutifully opened her mouth, reverently closed her eyes and received the small wafer on her tongue. Then she closed her mouth carefully – teeth were not supposed to contact the Host – and making quite sure not to bite Him, swallowed God.

Back in her place, Isabella gave herself up to contemplation. There was God, inside her, sitting on the tablecloth of her soul. Sister had said that now was the time to talk to Him and to pray. Isabella, not having anything in particular she could think of to say to Him, prayed a little and then remembered that at this moment she should be feeling supremely happy. She squeezed her eyes even more tightly shut and tried to force happiness upon herself. She felt disappointingly the same, though perhaps a little more holy. She opened her eyes and glanced down the row at her companions. They all had their eyes shut but they didn't look particularly happy. They looked just the same. But perhaps they were supremely happy inside. Perhaps once again Isabella was the odd one out. Perhaps the happiness started later. There was no way of knowing.

When Mass was over they went out into the sunshine, to the kisses and congratulations of their parents, to the smiles of Father and the Sisters and to the special breakfast which all the girls had looked forward to for days. Isabella, overexcited and over-tired by the events, found to her disappointment that she was not hungry. And so it went on for the rest of the day.

The much predicted and longed-for happiness never did arrive for Isabella on that special day, the day of her First Communion. It remained tantalizingly out of reach like the yellow roses climbing on the trellis by the chapel gate. Though she did reach another milestone on that day. It being Sunday, Father had to leave them, to celebrate another Mass at his own church. Tall and manly amongst so many females he was the focus of everyone's attention, particularly the Sisters, but as he left he turned and gave Isabella a special smile. "I am different," thought Isabella, for the first time with pride – an arrogance thus begun which was to dog her for the rest of her days.

COLD-BLOODED MURDER

IT'S NOT often that I stumble over a dead body but I did so, it was indeed the very first time, on that strange rainy Thursday afternoon, I am a writer, a mystery writer, a writer of murder and mayhem but never did it occur to me that I would find myself confronting the bloody reality, the reality about which I write so airily, so confidently. It was a weird feeling, a frightening, yet almost exciting feeling, particularly as I recognised the corpse – for corpse it undoubtedly was, as the large concave wound in its forehand, spilling blood and brains onto the footpath, testified. A bloody murder and on my own doorstep.

I live in Birchgrove, not on the waterfront nor on one of those fashionable streets where the trendy advertising men, the rich writers, artists and the ex-prime ministers and politicians live but at the other end – the less prosperous end. My late Victorian terrace house is one of the many lined up like toast in a rack along the spine of the ridge. Two bedrooms and an ancient bathroom upstairs, a larger living room with a fire place that really works on the ground floor and a damp basement that tends to flood in the occasional torrential summer rains we get on the coast. To that end my collection of wines sleep in racks high up, safely out of reach of the water.

I live alone, that is without human company. My company is a small black poodle named Lily who, as a congenial companion, is a great improvement on my late wife. I say "late" wife only in the sense that she is gone from me, she is not actually dead. Did a bunk with her personal trainer – a big guy, well sun-lamp bronzed with a fat golden chain spanning his massive throat – a throat I couldn't have got my hands around even had I wanted to. He was good at lifting heavy weights, slicking his long, blonde-streaked hair back with his fat fingers and licking his lips lewdly whenever he looked at my wife. She admired him unreservedly – that was the kind of girl she turned out to be and in the end I wasn't sorry to see the back of her. I comforted myself with the knowledge that I was not the first nor even the last to make such a foolish error of judgement.

The poodle was her legacy to me – she abandoned her too when she ran off with the gorilla.

I had always maintained that a poodle was a sissy sort of dog but left without my wife's hysterical cossetings and alone with me, I found otherwise. Lily is a dog with plenty of brains and plenty of courage. A game little dog, a dog full of fun and a great companion. She sits on her rug when I'm writing, waiting patiently for playtime. She has a box full of her own toys, balls of all kinds, rubber rings, old slippers and her favourite – a lambswool steering wheel cover left behind by guess who. She carries its white snake-like coils about, gets me to throw it down the long hall for her to retrieve and when she tires of that lies with her head cradled on its softness. Most afternoons we walk together – down to the waterfront or in one of the many parks in our area. On the way home we often stop at the pub down the lane and round the comer from number 27, where I can down a beer or two and Lily is allowed to sit at my feet. Everyone likes her there, she's just another dog. You'd hardly know she was a poodle now because I keep her coat woolly like a lamb. No more fancy French poodle clips for her. We have a fine life together.

So on that rainy Thursday when I found nature imitating art in the form of the bleeding corpse of Terry Murphy, my neighbour at number 29, 1 was not surprised. Terry Murphy was a well-known crim, not big time, just your ordinary small time slime, a big burly violent man who had spent a good deal of his time in prison. Not nearly enough time away for Rosie his wife and their five children. He beat them all regularly and for no good reason except that he was generally drunk, argumentative and totally unreasonable. His prison terms were a blessed relief for the family, Rosie told me later, a respite from his unreasoning violence. By the time I moved into number 27 next door, the children were grown and had moved away. Only Rosie and her youngest daughter Maureen still lived at number 29 – and the unwelcome Terry when he was not incarcerated. Those weeks and sometimes years when Terry used number 29 as his base for hatching heinous crimes and taking out his inevitable failures and frustrations on his hapless family were a nightmare for Rosie, though later the children always rallied to her support after some of Terry's more serious transgressions. Despite their hazardous upbringing they were good kids and mostly quite successful in their own way. It was to Rosie's credit that none of them followed in their father's footsteps. I heard their history over many a cup of tea in Rosie's house; or a glass of wine in mine. We became good friends quite quickly and mainly because of Lily. Our two patches of garden adjoined and the fence not being poodle proof gave Lily many excuses to call on Rosie. Though when Terry was home Lily kept well away. She had received a gratuitous kick in the belly from Terry after one of his drinking bouts and had never forgotten the cowardly deed. Whenever she saw Terry a low growl would rise in her throat and then she would dart rapidly behind my legs for protection. As I said, she was not a stupid dog. Rosie too was not exactly dumb though sometimes when I heard those noises from next door I wondered why she had stayed with Terry for so long. Later I realised that Rosie was as securely trapped as any poor song bird in its cage. Where would she go if she left number 29, her home for thirty years? She had no means of support other than her pension and had no intention of forcing herself and her problems onto her children. She valued her independence and loved her house and the small patch of garden behind it where she grew colourful annuals like zinnias and marigolds as well as a small bed of fragrant herbs. Her sweet peas growing on the fence between our two gardens were a rainbow profusion of colour every spring. Inside/ the house was crammed full of mementos, nearly all made of china – jugs, mugs, horses, dogs, cats and shepherdesses. The old burgundy cut moquette three-piece lounge suite had hand embroidered (by Rosie) antimacassars on their backs and her fireplace was bricked up. Whoever would have found time to split wood and feed a fire? Certainly not the recalcitrant Terry. In front of the fireplace stood an old kerosene heater, her only and meagre source of warmth in the winter.

Sometimes Rosie came to visit me and to borrow books. She was a voracious reader now, now that she had more time. In her youth this pleasure had been denied her, not only because of the lack of opportunity but also because seeing to the children and avoiding Terry's greater excesses took up most of her time. She learnt to love all my own old favourites like Raymond Chandler, Dashiell Hammett, Agatha Christie and Dorothy Sayers, and the more modem writers like P. D. James, or Roald Dahl. Even Ed McBain and Elmore Leonard were not too bloodthirsty for her to stomach. Of course she did not really have much choice in reading matter – what else would I have in my library? Occasionally she picked up a book by one of our own Aussie crime writers – but always reluctantly. Derivative, she said, including you, she said. Rosie was nothing if not direct.

So there he lay in his own blood – Terry Murphy, husband of Rosie, father of five kids and I can't say I felt anything more than relief. His final resting place was on the wet pavement in the lane across the road from number 30 in our street and just around the comer from the pub. That was no doubt where Terry had spent the afternoon as there was a strong smell of alcohol emanating from his corpse. I pulled Lily away from where she was nosing curiously around his boots and hurried home to phone the cops. While I was explaining matters to our local sergeant I noticed Lily dropping something into her toy box. She often finds special things on our walks together and brings them home – a magpie's feather – (she is particularly fond of all feathers – so delicious to chew,) an empty drink carton perhaps and once even an abandoned tennis ball. All of which she sensibly deposits in her box to bring out later when she feels so inclined. After I had reported my grisly find I went to Lily's box and noted her own find. It was something quite different from the usual and after its exposure to the rain, rather damp. Its significance did not strike me until some time later.

I went next door to be with Rosie when the news was broken as it soon was. Don Walsh the sergeant was kind, he'd known Rosie and her travails for many years and tactfully did not fill her in on the gory details. Predictably there were a few tears – after thirty years together the end, the finality of death, brings the good times to mind, not the bad. Three of her children turned up that night to be with their mother, the others were abroad, so she asked me and Lily to stay with her too. There was a chicken in the oven – a big no. 20 – a bargain at the local Woollies that day, and plenty to feed us all, she told us proudly as she put more potatoes into the oven to roast. Maureen had made a big salad and I popped round to the pub and bought a bottle of whisky which warmed all our hearts while we waited for dinner and told stories about Terry – fairly nice ones, surprisingly, there were even a few. While Rosie carved the chicken I raided my cellar for a couple of bottles of an excellent Semillon which we drank and under its mellow sway were soothed enough to move on to other stories, other events, no longer the strange, but somehow welcome demise of Terry.

The coroner was duly informed and all the usual formalities obeyed. A murder had certainly been committed but by whom? A passing thug was Don the sergeants opinion – probably an old mate of Terry's who'd been conned by him once too often. All the usual hoodlums were rounded up but the police weren't able to make anything stick. The main flaw in any possible prosecution was the lack of a murder weapon – the proverbial blunt instrument, Don told me over a beer in the pub a few days later. No clues at all, on or around the body? I asked him. None. None that they had been able to find anyway. You're the detective he told me, you found the body what did you make of it? Was it perhaps one of his old mates, one who had been done in the eye by Terry? No – that was the police's first thought too. Most of his old associates, not that there were many of them left who weren't already in jail, had been checked out and exonerated. Could have been one of his kids I said, knowing by now that the ones who lived in Sydney all had alibis for that miserable Thursday afternoon. I wouldn't have dobbed any one of them in with the law for quids. Don wasn't impressed. They'd checked all that out too. As for me I had nothing further to contribute and I think in Don's eyes I turned out to be a bit of a failure at detecting.

In the end Terry's murder was put down to "Person or Persons unknown" and life in our street went on as before. Well, not quite as before. For Rosie life became a lot sweeter. She lost that forlorn, hunted look she had worn whenever Terry was around. She became calm and serene and looked ten years younger.

One day when we were sitting together in her front room drinking an excellent espresso – her son had given her a remarkable machine – I leant down and picked something up off the floor. Then 1 handed her a handkerchief.

"You dropped this I think Rosie. "She felt in her sleeve and then puzzled, said, "But mine's here – show me that... "She examined the hanky – the embroidered bluebell in one comer and said,

"It's certainly mine... but where did you... "

"It wasn't me Rosie, Lily found it. She found it beside Terry's body. "

Rosie had the grace to blush. She remained silent. I went on,

"Lily brought it home that afternoon and put it in her box. I found it before we came in to your place. You know I've never seen anyone except ladies of your age put hankies in their sleeves anymore – it's such an old-fashioned habit, if you'll excuse the term. In fact modem young ladies hardly ever use handkerchiefs these days – not with Kleenex tissues around. "

Rosie remained very still, not looking at me. I could see she was weighing up the evidence so to speak. I went on,

"How did you do it Rosie?"

"I think you already know how, "Rosie said slowly, "and I guess you know too, that if it wasn't for you maybe I never would have done it.

"I guess I can take that Rosie. "I said. "It's all there in black and white isn't it?

I'm pretty sure I know how it was done but I want you to tell it to me anyway – tell me all the details – confession is good for the soul. "

There was a bit of a silence and then Lily padded over to sit with her head on Rosie's feet as though she knew the effort Rosie was having to make. Then, with a deep sigh Rosie began.

"The night before, before... you know... it happened, Terry was in a particularly foul mood. He'd been drunk for almost a week, couldn't get any of his old mates to help him rob the local bank or such like – you know him and his crazy scams. Then when he came back from the pub he started in on me again. The usual abuse flowed, he hit me a couple of times, only on the arms so it wouldn't show and then he took my china shepherdess off the mantelpiece, the blue one with the little lamb at her feet, my favourite – the one Sam brought back from England for me. He held it high up in the air laughing fit to burst. I begged him to put it down but he just laughed and laughed, watching me all the time, watching the tears I couldn't control, torturing me in that mean cold-blooded way of his. Finally, when he'd had enough of the game he just flung my poor little shepherdess down to smash to smithereens on the floor. "Rosie sighed again, paused, then went on bitterly,

"You could say I was lucky he didn't smash it over my head – anyway soon after that he passed out as usual. Next day coming home through the lane I met him on his way back from the pub. I asked him to help me with the shopping – it was pretty heavy but all he did was to aim a kick at me. The street was slick with rain and in his drunken state he slipped and fell. There he lay on the ground in front of me, trying to get up and not managing to get; a foothold on the wet pavement. As I watched his futile efforts all I could think of was my beautiful shepherdess, broken beyond repair. Somehow, remembering that mean and spiteful thing he'd done to me was the last straw – the breaking point for me. So I broke him too – a frozen no. 20 chook is every bit as effective as a club... "and then Rosie smiled and looked sideways at me,

"... or a frozen leg of lamb. You see just at that moment when I was finally angry enough to retaliate, something suddenly came back to me – I remembered the frozen leg of lamb used as a weapon by the heroine in that story of Roald Dahl's and without another thought I wielded my chook!"

It was Terry who, in the past had often claimed that reading books was not only a waste of time (Rosie's – she should have been cooking or ironing or something equally useful) not only a waste of time but positively dangerous.

He said reading gave people silly ideas, filled them with foolishness, cluttered their minds with things they oughtn't to know.

How right he was.

LADY IN DISTRESS

LILY JUMPED up onto my bed with all the fluidity and grace only a small poodle can command. She settled herself with her head cradled on a cushion and waited for my next move. Her black eyes followed me intently as I threw my overnight bag onto the bed beside her and began to pack. She knew what was in store for her and didn't mind a bit.

I needed to do some research for my current novel, background stuff, the details and workings of the wine industry. The book was a murder mystery (my fifth) set in the Hunter Valley, a beautiful spot where the grapes grow and where the wine is made and bottled. Lily was to go to a kennel for the three or four days my research would take. Marion McKenzie, the owner of the establishment, has a wonderful way with dogs as well as a beautifully clean and roomy environment. She puts all the Small dogs together in a large run where there is grass as well as concrete and shady trees where they can sniff, play and do the things dogs do when they're together. Lily knows Marion well from the overnight sojourns she occasionally enjoys there. Once when I went to the States for a trip she was with Marion for six weeks. Now it is almost like a second home for her. She loves Marion and the girls who work for her almost as much as she loves me, which is saying something because poodles are notoriously hard to please.

As I went around my small terrace house, locking up, Lily followed me closely, her lead trailing behind her. She watched me shutting windows and putting the automatic light switches in place. Not that I have any very valuable possessions – the money a hack mystery writer earns is not exactly a fortune – a pittance rather, in fact subsistence only – but I do have a few paintings and some books I would hate to lose. Also my house though small, boasts a cellar of which I have made good use. The cache of good wine down there is my main concern. I locked the cellar door very carefully.

Lily followed me out of the front door, I slammed it, and there was Rosie my ancient neighbour and one of my most faithful fans, watering her violets in the patch of garden below her front window. I told her where I was going and she promised to keep an eye on my bit of the house. Our terrace houses in Birchgove are set as close as sardines in a can – a proximity which sometimes has its advantages. I waved Rosie goodbye and put my bag and the dog into the car.

My stay in the Hunter Valley was uneventful but productive from two points of view. My research was fruitful, I discovered a great deal about the making and bottling of wine of all colours and then, the boot of the car satisfyingly heavy with a couple of cases of wine, I drove back to the kennel to fetch Lily.

I parked the car under a tree and when one of Marion's young helpers saw me she extracted the ebullient poodle from the run Lily welcomed me as though I had been away for three weeks not three days – a welcome without laying any blame on me for her abandonment; such unconditional love is a dog thing – it is hardly ever to be found in humans. I put Lily's collar back on and we went in search of Marion. We found her in the office talking earnestly to a girl, an exceedingly pretty girl with tears on her face. The girl was dabbing at her eyes with a soggy handkerchief and when she saw me turned away, embarrassed. At her feet sat a small black and white dog who sprang to his feet when he saw Lily and greeted her effusively. Lily backed off a little but then seemed to recognise what I can only describe as a remarkable animal. His eyes bulged at Lily, giving true meaning to the elusive word "eye-balling". His miniature tail wagged fitfully, his whole body squirmed with joy and I realised then that his goggle eyes were a permanent disfigurement. I was looking at a Boston terrier. Lily gave some delicate and lady-like sniffs at his nose and graciously allowed herself to be adored.

Marion laughed and said, "These two are friends of long standing so I'd better introduce their masters. "The girl had stopped crying by now and was patting her dishevelled face and hair back in place. Her hair was long, sleek, and a deep shining burgundy colour – rather like that of a long deep glass of Hunter Shiraz of very recent memory. Her wet eyes were a wonderfully transparent green – "deep pools" came instantly to my mind. Her dog's name was Algy – her own name, Velma Bennet. That name, the unusual Christian one rang a bell in my mind but the memory did not connect until later.

"Well" said Marion, "I don't think you need a cab now Velma – I think you have a lift back into town right here. "I needed no further hint. After we had settled our accounts with Marion we popped the dogs in the back of the car and set off on the drive back to town.

Velma's story was an unhappy one. She had left Algy with Marion while she flew up to Surfers to visit her aged parents who had gone up there to sunshine land to live. According to Velma they were not really aged at all, merely retired and working hard at having a good time. When they weren't swimming and surfing they were playing golf and visiting friends for cocktails. Velma enjoyed her few days with them but on her return – disaster. Velma had found her apartment in Double Bay ransacked. This was the story she was relating to Marion when I arrived. No wonder the poor girl was crying. She had lost her CD player, her discs, her television set all of which are of course replaceable. But her biggest losses, the ones causing her so much anguish were the antiques her parents had given her when they, moved to Surfers. An 18th century drop front desk, a beautiful walnut gaming table and a pair of Georgian silver candlesticks. And to add insult to injury her car had been stolen as well. The police were making the usual investigations but held out little hope for the recovery of any of Velma's possessions. The strange aspect of her story was the fact that her apartment and garage were in a security building. How the burglars had achieved entry and how they had removed the goods was a mystery. However, it looked fairly likely that having gained entry they had simply loaded their loot into Velma's car, a small but sturdy station wagon and had then driven off into the night.

When we arrived in Double Bay, Velma invited us to come in for a cup of coffee, as well as water and dog biscuits for our small friends – an irresistible invitation. By now I was feeling not only sorry for Velma but was also increasingly attracted by her sorrowful little face framed by that marvellous wine tinted hair. I wanted to help her, I wanted to avenge the wrong that had been done her, above all I wanted to hold and comfort her.

Over coffee I told her the story of Lily's life – how my ex-wife (I stressed the "ex") had run off with her personal trainer, a muscle-bound gorilla and had dumped Lily and me. My biggest mistake, I took pains to impress upon Velma had been marrying the silly woman in the first place. Lily had been her dog and had always looked frightful, like a pampered, perfumed genuinely preposterous French poodle. Left alone and with no one to answer to, I had taken the bows out of Lily's hair, had thrown away the fake jewelled collar and soon the weird hair-cut that had been forced on her had grown out and had left her looking like a proper dog and not like a circus act. Then I asked Velma to tell me Algy's story; at this important point in our brief relationship I did not want to dwell further on my own. Algy had been given to Velma by her parents before they had left for sunnier climes. They did not want her to live alone and without protection,

"Though how much protection I would get from Algy, "Velma said, "is questionable. He just loves everybody. Mind you he can look very fierce and maybe that's all I need. "

As Velma and I talked, Lily and Algy were racing through the now rather empty apartment having a fine time. Velma had given them both a bone shaped dog biscuit and while Algy instantly devoured his, Lily had buried hers under the pillows on the sofa, with Velma's permission of course.

Soon the afternoon became evening and Velma and I were still talking. We had looked into each other's eyes quite a bit and I did not feel inclined to go home. Nor, it seemed, did Velma want me to go. But the dogs needed walking so we took them down to the nearby park

Velma's apartment house was not enormous. It had been an old Victorian mansion, converted into units by a clever developer. Four in all, on two levels, with garages added in what had been the basement. I asked her about the other tenants, in particular whether anyone had seen or heard anything at all unusual while she was away. Velma was on good terms with them – they were good neighbours and she had spoken to them all.

Number three upstairs was occupied by a Miss Goodrich, a spinster in the real meaning of the word. She was a lady who had looked after her aged mother until the old woman died (at 96) and then had been forced to sell the family home and move into something smaller. She spent most of her days going backwards and forwards to the local library, that is when she wasn't at the local church either worshiping, doing the flowers, raising money by organising fetes or (in the main) bothering the vicar. She had not seen or heard anything unusual and neither had her cat. In number four upstairs lived the retired managing director of a shonky (so Velma surmised) company who entertained a lot though fairly quietly. He and his friends played a good deal of bridge. His cat had not seen or heard anything either. I gathered that the body corporate of the building was entirely happy about tenants owning pets. According to Velma Algy did not give the cats a hard time – he was as gentle as a lamb with both of them. The fourth occupants, on the same floor as Velma were a couple of old-fashioned lesbians. Old-fashioned in the sense that they were not by any means new age – no weird haircuts or body piercing here. The older of the two, plump and in her middle fifties was known as Auntie May, wore well cut tweed suits and sensible shoes and always drove the car. Her companion, Auntie Dorrie was younger, thinner, wore lots of blue eye shadow and Liberty shirtmaker dresses covered in rose buds with a matching cardigan always hanging around her shoulders. They went in for budgerigars and fish in tanks. They had been away at the same time as Velma,

"A few days in Katoomba – the air is like champagne you know, "said Auntie Dorrie and thus they had not been able to help the police with their inquiries. The said police seemed to be at a dead end and, declared Velma, tears welling again, could clearly care less. By now it was quite late and after making promises to Velma I doubted I could keep – that I would find the thief or thieves and return her belongings, Lily and I drove home. We found our little house secure, no invasion by burglars and after I had carefully stored my wine in the cellar we went off to bed.

Next day I called on my neighbour Rosie and told her Velma's sad story.

Rosie, an aficionado of crime, mystery and murder literature was a very astute lady. Often, when stuck on a plot development in one of my own thrillers, Rosie had come to the rescue. And it was not only in fiction that she lent support, in real life too her advice had often been invaluable. Her imagination was prodigious and her reasoning ingenious. She listened carefully and pouring me another glass of the good burgundy I'd brought her, said with some conviction,

"After what you've told me I bet anything you like this is an inside job. I suggest you call on the three other tenants and hear what they have to say. It wouldn't hurt to look around their units while you're there, and see what you can see. "

It did not take me long to act on Rosie's suggestion. There was also the not unpleasant prospect of seeing Velma again. I phoned and Velma agreed to set up appointments with the tenants. I told her to introduce me as a private detective who was looking into the robbery for her. Nature imitating my own art I told myself smugly.

The first appointment was with Colonel Fitzharding. We found him doing the weekly bridge problem in the newspaper but he put it down immediately, greeted us effusively, as did his huge tabby cat, and pressed us to a glass of sherry which we accepted. He was delighted to answer all my questions and agreed that the police had been absolutely hopeless in the matter of Velma's robbery, interviewing him for a mere five minutes. I took him back to the night of the fifteenth and he told us in long and boring detail his movements of that evening and night. He had been out to a bridge evening, a 6 O'clock start, at which time he and his friends played a couple of rubbers, then had a light dinner and played some more – usually till about eleven. He had driven into his garage, had seen the light on in Velma's garage although the door was shut and supposed that she had also just arrived home. It was only later he remembered that Velma was away in Queensland. He had told this fact to the police but nothing had come of it. Then the Colonel having nothing further to offer told us a few questionable jokes after which we left him to his bridge problem.

The two Aunties were extremely affable. They welcomed us and our two dogs with offers of coffee, water, biscuits and carrot cake. Their budgerigars tweeted and said "Pretty Boy" while I asked the questions. They repeated their story that they had been in the mountains, breathing in the good clean air, while Velma was away and therefore were unable to help. As I was munching on a slice of carrot cake Lily suddenly sat up, twitched her nose in an inquiring manner and ran out of the room. When I called her and she did not return I excused myself and hurried after her. I found her scratching on one of the bedroom doors trying to get in. I picked her up and returned to the sitting room.

"There must be something that interests Lily in there. "I said, "what could it be?"

"I can't imagine" Auntie May said "it's only my niece staying with us for a few days. She said she'd leave us to it when we knew you were coming. "

We gave up on the Aunties and went upstairs to see Miss Goodrich. The lady was voluble on the subject of burglaries in general and Velma's burglary in particular. Although she had seen and heard nothing on that fateful night (being slightly deaf) she had a theory which she gave us in detail. She maintained that the robbery was the work of a gang who dealt in antiques, first stealing, then selling them to rich Oriental's abroad, Japan in the main. The way to catch them was to set a trap. She would be glad to let us use her apartment for the execution of this ingenious plot. Her apartment was in fact stuffed with antiques. There was hardly room to swing her black and white cat, who's usual reclining area seemed to be on top of the baby grand piano. How we were to inform this gang of the kind invitation to fall into such a trap was a difficulty she had not foreseen. But I liked her spirit and it was quite clear she had nothing to do with the events of the fifteenth.

We returned to Velma's apartment and opened a bottle of champagne. It seemed the least we could do. After an hour or so, an hour in which I comforted Velma in the best way I knew, holding her close and whispering in her ear, it was time to take the dogs for a walk. It seemed Rosie's theories had come to nought, unlike my progress with Velma.

"But why did Lily scratch at that door?" asked Velma as we strolled along the waterfront. It was something I had forgotten until then, since it hadn't seemed important at the time, but the more I thought about it the more certain I became that the incident deserved further investigation.

"I have no idea," I told her, "but we're going back to have another look." I trust the instincts of my little dog – something unusual was in there I'm sure of it.

Auntie Dorrie opened the door to our knock and immediately Lily shot past her and dashed into the sitting room. We followed and found her jumping up and licking a pretty young woman who was sitting on the sofa. Algy followed and did the same. The young woman was patting the excited dogs but quite reluctantly and looking distinctly dismayed.

"Hello Kylie," I said "so you're the absent niece. Lily is very pleased to see you, so is Velma and so are Algy and I." By this time Velma and the two Aunts were looking decidedly bemused. I went on,

"Well now Kylie I guess you could tell us a thing or two about Velma Bennet's antiques could you not?"

Kylie burst into tears and after the whole wretched story emerged the two Aunties did likewise.

Kylie is one of Marion McKenzie's helpers at the kennel and so knew that when Velma left her dog there her apartment would be empty. Kylie told us, still tearfully that her boyfriend seeing his chance, had persuaded her to ask her Aunt. whether she could stay in their apartment while they were away in Katoomba to feed the fish and the birds. And there you are – Bob's your Uncle. Easy and unlimited access to Velma's flat – her credit card accessible lock would have to be changed – Velma's furniture and little or no chance that anyone would come up with the connection. Indeed the police had not done so. Full of remorse Kylie dobbed in the crooked boyfriend, vowing never to transgress again and certainly to have nothing further to do with the now incipient jailbird.

In the end Kylie only received a good behaviour bone} and the Aunties promised to keep her on the straight and narrow from now on. Even Marion Mckenzie took her back at the kennel on her promise to be good and keep her mouth shut about the client's movements.

Velma's car and furniture were recovered entirely intact. The boyfriend had hardly had time to unpack the goods, much less fence them.

And it was, as Velma later said all due to the clever little shiny black nose of Lily.

Velma also said that she could never thank me enough for all I had done. But I can vouch for the fact that she certainly gave it a good try.

GETTING RID OF SYL

I WAS SITTING with my friend Rosie in our garden sipping an excellent Hunter Valley Burgundy and watching the, for once, pollution-free sunset when it happened. I say "our garden" because Rosie is my next door neighbour in the bank of terraces in Birchgrove in which we live. The houses are set as close as honeycombs in a hive (and buzz like bees with gossip) and each one has a tiny garden at the back. After Rosie's husband died we agreed to remove the dividing fence so that Lily, my black poodle could have a bigger space in which to play. It has worked beautifully because as well as more room I have a lovely view and the scent of Rosie's extensive herb and flower garden. So there we were, sipping companionably, enjoying the colourful dying of the day, a particularly spectacular sight that evening. The horizon was full of overblown, billowing dark clouds tinged with a doom-laden crimson. A portent. as it turned out. of what was to come. Lily sat at our feet quietly adoring her favourite squeaking toy, a black and white soccer ball, when, as I said, it happened - a loud knocking on my front door, easily heard in the garden, accompanied by an equally loud shouting of my name. I ran to the door and there she was, Sylvia my ex-wife. She stood on the doorstep, a bag in her hand and in that same plummy, entirely unchanged voice of hers, proclaimed hysterically,

"Darling – Rudi has done the dirty on me, landed me in the most awful goddam mess - I simply don't know where to turn." I was extremely surprised not to say displeased that she had turned to me, however I led her inside and said quietly,

"Calm down Syl – we'll go and sit in the garden and you can tell me all about it."

"Don't call me Syl..." she snarled as of yore, "my name is Sylvia." And then it all came back to me - how it had been for most of the two years in which she had made my life a misery. The invitation to the garden was a diversionary tactic. My mind was already in high gear attempting to figure out a foolproof scheme for ridding myself of the awful Syl as quickly as humanly possible.

In the garden Rosie looked at Syl with open disapproval (her memory was as good as mine) and muttered a perfunctory greeting. Next, Lily, after one look at the woman who had once been her mistress, ran upstairs with her ball, probably to hide under my bed. I was sure she had not forgotten her agonising visits to the Poodle parlour where she had been trimmed and teased into the most fanciful and uncomfortable shapes ever devised by man. Syl, her nose out of joint because Lily had not fallen over herself to recognise her, had in fact ignored her, said disdainfully:

"Whatever have you done to that poor animal? She looks a fright, like a scruffy black sheep, not like a proper French poodle at all. I never should have left her with you, I might have known you'd neglect her."

"That's how she likes to look," I said "and how I like her to look. Now get on with it – what's the problem?"

My initial sympathy for her situation was beginning to fade as fast as snow melting in spring sunshine. Syl smoothed her counterfeit golden locks, solid with hairspray, and said a little more congenially,

"I'd love some of that vino darling, it might settle my nerves." Rosie produced another glass and unwillingly – it was really an excellent burgundy – I poured. Syl swallowed the wine in one gulp and held out her glass for more. Rosie and I exchanged glances and shuddered.

"Well darling," began Syl "you'll never guess what's happened. It's more weird than you could ever imagine or even dream up to write about in those deadly boring little thrillers of yours."

My writing of mystery stories and the poor returns these engendered had always been the bone of contention that had stuck deep in Syl's throat. So much so that she had left me for a muscle-bound orangutans who ran a gym for ladies who needed to rid themselves of extra kilos. He was a big guy, sunlamp bronzed with a massive throat I couldn't have got my hands around even had I wanted to. Syl admired him unreservedly - that was the kind of girl she turned out to be and in the end I wasn't sorry to see her go. However it seems this intellectual giant had quickly tired of her extravagances and had thrown her out. Next in line came Rudi, who, as it seemed now, had also found her less than alluring. He was the psychotherapist who was supposed to sort her out after her disappointment. I heard on the grapevine that she had moved in with him – now, clearly, something had changed.

"Rudi..." moaned Syl, desperately raking scarlet ceramic fingernails through her metallic coiffure, "...has killed someone and framed me for the murder." Rosie and I exchanged further glances, this time of disbelief.

My friend Rosie was an old hand at the inequities of life. Her husband had been clubbed to death outside his favourite pub, a fitting end for the bully and drunkard that he was. Rosie's lifestyle had improved no end since his demise. She was able to do as she pleased, working in her garden or reading the crime fiction she loved. We had a great neighbourly relationship which included my often asking for help when stuck on a fine detail of plot. Now she gave Syl one of her deceptively bland looks that hid a quick intelligence and asked.

"What have you been drinking my dear?"

"I'm not your dear and I'm not drunk you silly old crone," said Syl – tact was not a quality with which she had been endowed, "Why can't you believe me, it's true, you'll read it in the papers tomorrow." Rosie did not flinch at the insult, she knew Syl of old.

"Rudi borrowed my car, well, our car, but it's in my name." Syl wasn't born yesterday – everything was always in her name, as I had discovered to my cost. She went on,

"He was driving back from lunch with a friend, he told me, when he ran over a woman crossing the road in Double Bay. Because he knew he was over the limit, (he'd had quite a few drinks with lunch,) he didn't stop, and drove on home. Then he said he was leaving me, said that he was giving me notice that if charged he would deny everything and tell the police that I was driving the car. It gets worse..." Syl went on mournfully, "... he said the woman was quite probably dead and that I could be charged with manslaughter." At this point Syl broke down and wept piteously. Rosie, ever solicitous, handed her a handkerchief. and encouraged her to continue.

"He told me that what he was doing was fair enough. He had the hide to say that since I'd always charged everything I ever bought to him and made him practically bankrupt – which is a rotten lie – it was now my turn to be charged."

He had a keen sense of humour did Rudi. I began to experience a kind of fellow feeling for him.

By now the sun had set and mosquitos were out and hunting so we moved inside.

We found Lily lying on her rug and making herself as invisible as possible. She shrank even more when she saw Syl, but stood her ground like the brave little dog she was. She trusted me, She knew I wouldn't hand her back to Syl to be tormented. Syl threw herself into a chair still sniffing and wiping her eyes, whined,

"So now I can't go home or I'll be arrested and there's simply no-one else I can trust so I came here."

"You've thrown yourself on our mercy," said Rosie, who thought of my troubles as her own.

"I guess so," Syl admitted reluctantly and sniffed some more.

I've got a spare room," Rosie said generously, "you can stay with me till we work something out."

I breathed a sigh of relief. The thought of Syl back in my little house, bawling at Lily and me and causing her former havoc was too much to contemplate. Syl stopped sniffing and thought the offer over. After weighing the non-existent alternatives she came up with the only reply,

"Oh well – I suppose that will have to do." Tactful to the last our Syl. The problem remained. Rosie's and mine, how to get rid of Syl and soon.

In bed, I thought the situation over. First of all could we believe Syl's story? She had been a liar from way back, bending the truth to suit herself. Perhaps she had herself committed the hit-and-run and was now hiding from the police. On the other hand, were we to believe Syl there was something in Rudi's alleged story that didn't make sense. It was too pat, too simple. It smacked of premeditation. Could it be that Rudi was not only guilty of a hit-and-run accident but guilty of murder, guilty of a deliberate plot to frame Syl in order to get rid of her? I could relate to that. Similar thoughts had floated about in my mind before she had taken the matter out of my hands and left me. This scenario intrigued me, and next morning over coffee and hot croissants, I discussed it with Rosie. Syl was still heavily asleep in bed, a break for the three of us. We agreed that supposing Syl had told the truth there was every chance that what Rudi had done was no accident.

The papers arrived just as we were finishing breakfast and sure enough on page four there was a short paragraph headed,

HIT AND RUN

Yesterday afternoon in Double Bay an unidentified woman was hit by a black BMW on a pedestrian crossing. The car did not stop. The woman was pronounced dead on arrival at St. Vincent's Hospital. Police inquiries are continuing.

"Not much to go on but could support our theory," I remarked. Rosie said thoughtfully,

"In the interests of getting rid of Syl why don't you pay Rudi a visit and see what ticks?"

Unwillingly, since I did not want to confront a potential criminal, I agreed. It is one thing to write about nefarious doings, quite another to face the reality. I poured another cup of coffee to strengthen my resolve while Rosie disappeared indoors. After a few minutes she returned.

"I've made an appointment for you with Dr. Rudolph Strum the eminent psychotherapist," said Rosie, who was often way ahead of me,

"He is a very busy man but decided to fit you in today after hearing your sad story."

"My sad story?"

"Yes very sad – you're quite ill or should I say mentally challenged."

"Why?" I asked

"Your wife left you for another man, a richer man, didn't she?" Rosie's sense of humour could be irritating,

"and left you utterly bereft. Your name for the purpose of this exercise is Philip Marlowe."

Rosie always thought of everything.

I arrived at Rudi's office to discover the place in turmoil. The police had overrun it and had Rudi in a flap. I took the opportunity to look around his waiting room. There were various soothing paintings on the walls, yachts sailing on calm blue seas and pale flowers in vases. No Brett Whiteleys here to confuse the already confused. There were also two framed diplomas which I examined carefully. They pronounced that Dr Rudolph Strum was proficient in the twin arts of Psychology and Psychiatry and had received these diplomas which said so. The certificates were heavily embossed and had been issued, said the very small print at the bottom, in Dubuque, Iowa U.S.A which presumably had a famous school of Psychiatry. You could have fooled me.

After the police left, Rudi showed me into his inner sanctum, a dark heavily-panelled room with two comfortable armchairs on either side of a faux marble fireplace. On his huge shiny desk stood two bronze busts facing each other and instantly recognisable – one of Freud and one of Jung. Rudi was clearly a man who kept his options open. He waved me to a chair and, taking up a clipboard and pen, sat down in the other one. For a man who called himself a psychotherapist I felt he did not have the presence the term suggested. His eyes were far too close together and his mandatory beard too sparse – unlike the luxuriant growth on the Freudian bust decorating his desk.

"Now Mr. Marlow," he began, "I must apologise for the commotion here this morning but I've sorted it all out now."" I enjoyed being called Mr. Marlowe. It made me feel more like a true private eye and I must admit instilled a little more courage into my cowardly breast.

"Well Mr. Marlowe, or may I call you..." he consulted his notes, "Philip. Tell me all about your problems, Do not feel shy or intimidated I beg of you – I am here to help. "

Rudi spoke with the slightest of accents, an accent hard to place since it was clearly assumed, but his voice was deep and warm and pitched to inspire confidence. I admired his equanimity for a man who had earlier been under scrutiny from the police. But he seemed to me to be too cool, too together. I thought his self-possessed behaviour was further evidence in favour of his guilt. It smacked of premeditation.

I spun him the story Rosie and I had concocted and he was suitably condoling. To his credit he did not reveal by a single yawn that he'd heard it all before. Just before my time was up he introduced the subject of his fee. Money, I knew from hearsay, was a favourite topic amongst psychotherapists and their patients. They insinuate that it's part of the treatment, that in some way one will feel better after being parted from ones hard-earned. He explained that he dealt in cash only - no bills. I agreed to pay the inordinate amount he specified, intending, by hook or by crook to get it back from Syl later. Rudi didn't know it yet, but this had been my first and last appointment. I was put outside to pay his secretary, a nubile blonde who looked so young I wondered if she could read and write. I paid her in cash and asked for a receipt.

"Dr. Strum doesn't believe in receipts," she told me, rolling her blue eyes innocently.

Surprise, surprise.

"You are an incredibly pretty girl," I told her, "why aren't you on the stage, why aren't you in movies – what keeps you working for him?" I indicated Rudi "s door. She giggled prettily,

"It's just a job I guess."

"You're too good for it," I said, giving her my best cool Marlowe twinkling of the eyes. She giggled again.

"Tell me something," I went on "how long has Dr. Strum been practising in this country –– I see his diplomas are from the States? "

"Oh I wouldn't know - I only work here." She gave me another giggle.

"Do the Strums live on the premises?" I asked.

"Oh sure, upstairs." She became expansive.

"The police were here this morning looking for Mrs. Strum. She's missing you know. They think she did that hit-and-run. She could be up for manslaughter." She giggled again – her principal means of communication it seemed. I left her to it.

Back in Birchgrove I found Rosie and Lily digging in the garden and Syl indoors lounging in front of my television set watching a daytime soap.

"Tell me Syl," I began,

"Don't call me Syl," she hissed.

"Sylvia, did you actually marry Rudi or did you just move in with him?"

"Of course I married him - I wasn't going to be a mere defacto like I was with Trev. Trev was the orang-utan.

"I learnt a lot from Trev," she went on "the bastard left me high and dry and totally broke."

"I thought you already knew all about that," I said mildly which was nevertheless a mistake. I had unleashed a terrible diatribe. When at last I could get a word in I said,

"That's enough muck-raking Syl, if you don't shut up, I'll throw you to the cops, and good riddance." It worked. She shut up.

Rosie and I decided we had reached an impasse. What to do next? Would we be stuck with Syl forever? The thought was unbearable.

But next morning there was a development. We read in the paper that the victim of the hit and run in Double Bay had been identified as Mona Mereweather (54) of Woollahra.

"My God." cried Syl, "she's in one of Rudi's work groups – hey meet once a month to discuss their cases. Mona was a weird ugly old bat and moronic as well." Syl's assessment of human character had never been astute – primitive was how I would put it.

"But perhaps Mona was clever as well," said Rosie, "what if she was blackmailing Rudi and so he killed her?"

Syl, her face flushed and angry, came in with a non-sequitur.

"I'm going to kill that bastard when I get my hands on him – I'll kill him, I swear it..." Her voice climbed an octave "how dare he frame me for a murder he committed – he just wants to get rid of me so he can run off with that little tart he uses as a secretary. Secretary, what a joke, she can hardly read and write" I was pleased to have my reading of the giggling girl's abilities confirmed. Syl went on "and after I gave him the best years of my life too." Wisely I held my tongue.

The next two days were unproductive. Rosie was remarkably patient with Syl who, deprived of her life blood, her very raison d'etre – shopping – had become even more sullen and bad tempered. Unable to prowl the shops using Rudi's money she either snarled at Rosie, at Lily or at me, that is when she wasn't watching television. Her hair, without its twice weekly visit to the hairdresser had turned on her. In fact both Syl and her hair looked ready to snap. Dark roots showed through the wiry, yellow unkempt strands – she looked a mess. Not even the acres of jangling jewellery she wore to cheer herself up, helped to liven up her appearance.

Lily had become used to her alien presence in our lives. She didn't like it much but behaved, if not with her usual ebullient exuberance at least with restraint and kept out of Syl's way as much as possible.

The evening came when I was forced to visit my accountant - a crucial visit as my tax return was overdue. He had three cats, a vile temper and consistently refused Lily entry into his house. Unfortunately Rosie was away visiting one of her children so I had no choice but to leave Lily with Syl. Unwillingly. I was away about three hours. When I returned Syl was in Rosie's sitting room watching a game show. Lily was not to be seen.

"Where's Lily?" I asked anxiously.

"That bloody dog," replied Syl indifferently, "I locked her in your house — she was barking so much I couldn't hear the television. "That was a lie for sure, Lily was not a barker for no reason. Briefly I wondered what Syl had been up , and hurried home.

I found Lily sitting quietly on her rug, chewing a bedraggled piece of pink ribbon, something she had probably picked up at Rosie's. She appeared quite unharmed, fortunately, since one never knew with Syl. I went to bed feeling virtuous about my tax and wondering just how long we could continue to put up with the frightful Syl. But our ordeal was about to come to a surprising end.

Next morning on the radio came the bombshell.

"Early this morning the body of Dr. Rudolph Strum was found in his office. He died as a result of a single blow to the head. Nothing was disturbed; the police suspect foul play and investigations are under way." I leapt out of bed, threw on jeans and a shirt and dashed next door. Rosie and Syl were sitting in the kitchen drinking coffee and chatting quite amiably for a change. I broke the news. Syl paled but recovered quickly.

"Serves him right – the swine!" She used the old-fashioned epithet with relish.

"Syl," I asked quietly, "where were you last night?" Syl looked shaken, then her voice rose to a shriek,

"What do you mean you idiot – do you think I killed him? You must be out of your mind..." At which point Lily growled and snapped at her – protecting me from the enemy.

"As for that damn dog, she'll have to be put down, she's dangerous, she's a killer."

Strange, I thought, that Lily was suddenly so volubly anti Syl, why?

"Answer the question Syl, where were you last night?"

Before she could reply, we heard loud knocking coming from my house. I looked out of Rosie's window and there were the police, two of them, one fat, one thin, standing at my door.

"Stay here and stay quiet," I ordered Syl, and, taking Lily with me, returned home.

It seemed the trail had finally led the police to me, the ex-husband, seeking Syl.

She was wanted for both murders.

"What's the motive?" I asked. "Money - the Doctor was insured for a million dollars."

"And the woman?"

"We're not sure," admitted the fat one "but we can tell you this, Rudolph Strum was an alias. His real name is Wayne Foster, a Melbourne psychiatrist who was struck off the register some years ago, for molesting a patient – female," he added helpfully.

"Don't tell me," I said, "then he went to the States and purchased a couple of spurious degrees.: It was all beginning to fall into place. Except for Syl's part in the mystery.

I assured the police that Syl was certainly not in my house and vowed to help if I possibly could.

"Looks like my theory was correct," said Rosie later as she put more coffee on.

"Mona Mereweather must have been blackmailing Rudi knowing that he had been struck off."

"Which would certainly have prevented him from practising," I said. "plenty of motive there for murder."

"Now that I come to think of it," said Syl, "Rudi had some extra meetings alone with that ugly old tart. One time I heard raised voices. I would have gone down to see what they were up to but I'd just done my nails." Syl's priorities were always firmly in place.

Lily growled at her again. My sentiments exactly, though Lily's sudden hatred of Syl needed an explanation. It was not like my happy little dog to be so cantankerous.

Rosie poured coffee and said

"If we are correct there must be something, somewhere, in writing." I sighed.

"I suppose that means you want me to go looking for evidence?" Rosie and Syl nodded.

"O.K. but..."

"Oh, sorry but you can't do that – his room is a crime scene. Did you know..." her voice became hushed, "... he was killed by a blow on the head from that bust on his desk – the one with the beard – isn't that awful...?" She meant ironic - a word probably not in her vocabulary.

"Really awful," I smiled again. My face was becoming quite stiff with all my false hilarity.

"Can't you help me at all – it's really important." I was begging now with my best pleading crooked smile.

"Well there's some stuff over there with the newspapers which Dr Strum asked me to burn." She indicated a bundle in the corner tied up with string.

"Ready for recycling?" I asked.

"Yes – how did you know?" she looked impressed.

"Just guessing," I told her and broke the string.

It didn't take long to find what I wanted – two letters, helpfully signed by Mona Mereweather telling Rudi that what he was doing was unethical and unless he stopped practising she would be obliged to tell the authorities. Not blackmail as such. then, merely a busybody who had stuck her nose into Rudi's business and had paid the price. I left blondie with one last grateful smile.

Home once more and Lily was so pleased to see me she almost jumped out of her skin. Syl was sulking in her bedroom, which left Rosie and me delightfully alone.

Rosie read the letters through and said, "Well – one murder more or less proved but who killed Rudi? Do you think Syl could have done it? "

"Not really – she's all talk."

"But she hated him enough," replied Rosie, "never underestimate the power of a woman's vengeance. Where was she that night anyway – did she ever tell you?"

"No, she didn't – she was supposed to be here looking after Lily, and when I got home here she certainly was."

"But you were away for three or more hours – plenty of time for Syl to get to Rudi, smash his head in with his bronze mentor and be back before we returned. He was definitely murdered by someone he knew, since there was no evidence of a struggle." Rosie was beginning to convince me.

We confronted Syl. She suddenly transformed herself from the strident, shrewish virago into the poor little misunderstood victim.

"Darling – for heaven's sake, I didn't murder Rudi. God knows I hated him in the end but I didn't kill him, I really didn't, I swear it darling." She essayed a few crocodile tears.

"Come on Syl, tell us, where you were the night Rudi was murdered."

"Never you mind – that's my own business."

"It's police business Syl – they'll get you for Rudi's murder unless you have a solid alibi."

Syl looked positively embarrassed, a rare look, one I had never seen on her face before. I felt sure the truth was about to emerge. Syl wrung her hands,

"Well...after you both left I was bored. I wanted to make Lily look nice – she looks such a fright – anyway I found a ribbon in Rosie's sewing basket, brushed Lily, and then I was putting the ribbon on her topknot when..."

"When what?" More wringing of hands. I could see what was coming.

"When she attacked me – she bit me – that dog is a killer." Rosie and I burst out laughing.

"Where did she bite you?" Syl held out her left hand. Wrapped around the little finger was a band aid.

"That tiny little bruise is your alibi?"

"It "s more than a bruise, she pierced the skin with her huge teeth and there was blood, lots of blood." Syl was an old hand at exaggeration.

"But that doesn't prove you were here at home while Rudi was being murdered." Syl looked even more shifty.

"Well..." she was finding it difficult to spit it out.

"...I locked Lily in the house and went round to the local doctor to get a tetanus shot."

Rosie and I were too flabbergasted to speak.

"Well darling one can't be too careful with that dirty dog digging in the garden all day She wouldn't have been allowed to do that in my day. "

"In your day the dog wasn't a dog she was a shampooed, perfumed toy."

Syl ignored that, then self-righteously added,

"Anyway that creep of a doctor made me wait for ages in his awful waiting room full of the low life that live around here. I don't know how you put up with it."

With the help of Mona Mereweather's letters Syl was able to convince the police that she had not been driving the lethal BMW, and her alibi with the local doctor was easily proved. Thus exonerated, she packed her jangling bracelets, her nail polish, her industrial strength hair spray and begged me to move her back to her apartment' which I did with alacrity. She did not say goodbye to Lily, her saviour.

Finding Rudi's killer proved more difficult. The police remained baffled, but Rosie and I thought we had the answer. Given the irony of the murder weapon we knew it could only have been wielded by a dissatisfied patient. Having suffered briefly at Rudi's hands, I opted for a man. Rosie, true to her edict that women are big on vengeance, maintained that it could only have been a woman. We bet a bottle of Moet on the outcome, and after a mere six months the police announced a breakthrough. A woman, unable to live with her guilt had come forward and confessed to Rudi's murder. She had been a patient of Rudi's for two years and declared that the discussions about money which he insisted upon at the close of each session had finally driven her into a frenzy of fury and frustration. At the end of what was to be Rudi's last hour she had

picked up the bronze head of Sigmund Freud, meaning, she said, to throw it through the window but, and I quote: "Dr. Strum's head got in the way."

Put on trial for manslaughter the feisty and attractive woman was tried by a jury who deeply distrusted psychotherapists. She was put on a good behaviour bond, providing she agreed to undergo psychiatric care – another ironic touch with which I am sure the brave woman would be able to cope effortlessly.

I gave Rosie her bottle of bubbly which she shared with me one evening in our garden. We sat watching the sunset while Lily buried her own reward – a large and meaty bone intended for exhumation at a later date.

Of course the frightful Syl collected Rudi's insurance which I believe she is spending with an abandon some would call reckless. To date I am still trying to collect Rudi's fee from her. I don't hold out much hope. At least with Lily's help we finally got rid of Syl, worth rather more to me than the price of one short visit to a shady shrink.

THE CATS OF ALGECIRAS

IT WAS proposed that our visit to Tangier should be undertaken by ferry from Algeciras. It sounded exciting and since we were already in Spain, an excellent idea. The Euroferry ticket complete with views of Gibraltar and a surfacing whale added spice to the venture.

We drove from Cordoba, across the mountains, down to Malaga and then on a beautifully constructed freeway along the magnificent coast to Algeciras – romantically known as The Gateway to Africa.

We booked into our three star hotel, the Albian where we would spend the night and leave early the next morning for Tangier. Our car and luggage were to be left in the care of the hotel.

Our room was a modest one on the fourth floor and without the view of Gibraltar we had been expecting. Instead we looked out onto a road at the rear of the hotel and onto four huge green and rusty garbage bins below our window which obviously belonged to the hotel. Across the road we had a more pleasant view – many large houses of the well to do, with lush gardens, some with swimming pools and many with dogs, lots of dogs, loud, large and undefined in ancestry.

And under our window lived the cats of Algeciras. They were lean and active. Seven in number. One, clearly the mother of the brood was tan and white in colour and three of the cats were her kittens or rather as we surmised, teenagers. Not fully grown but not babies either. The others were perhaps relations, older sons and daughters, but certainly family as we soon saw. They varied in colour from black and brown, to black and white and tabby. How had they survived so long? They were lean but in good condition, their fur shiny and clean.

In the afternoon three boys aged about nine or ten came by on bicycles and began to harass the cats. They yelled and rang their bicycle bells, they barked like dogs to frighten the cats and these noises certainly made them run. All the cats made a dash for the nearest safety zone and disappeared behind an iron barred gate that led into an overgrown garden. Unafraid they peered out from behind the oleanders and burgeoning bougainvillea. They knew the boys could not follow them there. This was a game of sorts and had obviously been played out before. The boys rode on and soon the seven cats of Algeciras reappeared amongst the rubbish bins. We are strangely drawn to their plight. How have they survived so long? Doubtless the rubbish bins have a lot to do with their survival. We watched again as three of the family jumped onto the rims of two of the bins and gazed and assessed the rubbish therein. They were extremely agile sometimes even jumping into the depths of a bin which caused us to wonder whether they would ever be able to make their way out. We watched and suddenly with one lithe spring one jumped out. The others soon followed but without food of any kind – it seemed there was nothing there to eat just now. Perhaps after dinner the hotel will throw scraps into the bins. The kittens jumped and played, jumping as high as they can – practicing for the inside of the bins? Every now and again the mother cat jumped on one of them and licked it thoroughly all over. They played together, good-natured play, rolling, jumping and running together.

I rummaged in our picnic basket and found some scraps of cheese, mainly rinds and some old bits of mortadella. I threw it all down for them. Leaning out of the window we watched. At first no one noticed and then one cat found the meat. Remarkably he did not take it away to eat by himself as we expected. He stood guard over it, waited for the others, particularly the smaller ones and allowed them to eat first. We watched as the whole family shared the food. I found the remains of two papers in which butter had been wrapped. I threw both down. With great delight the kittens, delicately and with fervour licked up the butter – it was fascinating to watch as they took turns to lick – no greed at all despite their probable hunger. Was it their dependence on each other that secured their survival? Or could it be love for each other – a theory too farfetched it is true but seductive nevertheless.

Suddenly one black and white cat, a larger one looked up and saw me – his yellow eyes on mine. I threw down the remains of a bread roll, first breaking it into smaller pieces and another butter paper. Again, this cat, the only one to realise the origin of this manna from heaven looked up – what was it thinking? The family seized the bread and shared again, the small ones gnawed and ate while others delicately licked again at the butter on the paper.

The next day we set off for Tangier, taking the ferry past the "Crouching Lion" that is Gibraltar, a wonderful trip but that is another story.

On our return we spent one more night at the hotel Alboran and in the same room. We arrived in the late afternoon. Immediately I went to the window and looked for the cats. I was quite relieved to see them. I had worried that dogs or children, more boys on bikes, this time wielding rocks not screams had dispersed or even killed them. But no, there they were- the street cats of Algeciras in excellent form.

It is said that birds should not be fed in case they become reliant on the seed in the feeder and should the supply cease will be unable to fend for themselves. I have never been of that opinion though there may be some truth in the theory. Cats however are different are they not? From Tangier and our picnics there I brought back enough food for the seven delicate cats of Algeciras. We watched as they ate their fill, delicately, and sharing with each other as before. Afterwards when not a skerrick was left my friend, the black and white cat with the yellow eyes gazed up at me again. 1 like to think the look we exchanged was conspiratorial.

www.ingramcontent.com/pod-product-compliance
Lightning Source LLC
Chambersburg PA
CBHW052033260626
47163CB00006B/296